DESTROYING ANGEL

A FOX COUNTY FORENSICS NOVEL

CARA MALONE

Copyright © 2023 by Cara Malone

All rights reserved.

No part of this book may be reproduced in any form or by any electronic or mechanical means, including information storage and retrieval systems, without written permission from the author, except for the use of brief quotations in a book review.

1
JULIA

"*Earth to Julia!*"

She snapped out of her daydream, suddenly and uncomfortably aware that her new boss, Tom, had been calling her name – what now passed as her name – for some time. And the entire department was now staring at her.

Nightmare fuel.

"Sorry," the detective known as Julia Taylor responded, color flooding her fair cheeks.

"Are you a homicide detective or a space cadet?" one of her fellow new recruits, Renee Duvall, asked.

Ugh. She'd only been on the job for one week, mostly doing onboarding and other dull training materials, but she could already tell she and Renee were not destined to be work wives.

"Get enough sleep last night?" Julia's other boss, Arlen, asked. At least that seemed like a question born of genuine concern, but if she had it to do over again, Julia would have just answered to her damn name and avoided all this in the first place.

She was going to need more practice at that.

"I did, thanks," she said. "I was just... thinking about an article I read on narcotics-related deaths."

That was *not* what she was thinking about, but the article was real enough. She'd transferred to Fox County PD from Grand Rapids, Michigan, a city with a similar population size but a vastly different crime profile. There wasn't nearly the opiate epidemic there that Fox County was dealing with, and she'd been brushing up.

"Anything illuminating?" Tom asked.

"Well, less than one percent of all overdoses are homicides, so we probably won't be working many of those," Julia said. "But there are significantly greater instances of narcotics-driven violence, so we probably *will* see that type of scene often."

Tom looked unimpressed, but Arlen said, "Glad to see you're doing your homework on our population."

"Anyway," Tom said, "if we can get back to business..."

Julia's cheeks colored again at the reminder that she was to blame for the interruption.

"Taylor, you're going to be with me today," he said. *Oh, great.* "Duvall, you're with Detective Rose. And the rest of you – desk duty."

The other three new recruits clustered around Tom and Arlen's desks stifled groans, and Julia tried to suppress a smile at having been chosen on their first day on duty. Renee made no such attempt – she was grinning from ear to ear.

"What are we getting into, boss?" she asked Arlen.

"I'm in the middle of investigating a death reported as a slip-and-fall that turned out to be a homicide," she said. "We need to talk to the wife." She turned to the other three newbies. "You all can start looking through the open cases – see if you can close some of them."

Arlen left, Renee trailing after her, and Julia turned to Tom. "What about us?"

"We're on deck if a new call comes in," he said. "Otherwise, same as these grunts. Case review."

If the others objected to being called grunts, they didn't show it. Probably too damn grateful to be here to start complaining already.

All five of the new detectives were women, which by itself was a major upset to the status quo. And if Julia's gaydar was functioning properly, she was not the only queer one in the bunch. Even before she started thinking about getting a new job, she'd heard near-mythical tales of the police department in Pennsylvania that was not only LGBTQ+ friendly, but staffed largely with gorgeous queer women.

The promised land of policing.

Now that she was here, it was turning out to be every bit as true as the rumors said, and if her fellow new recruits were here for the same reason, they'd probably be happy to do all the grunt work in the world for the privilege of carrying a Fox County badge.

Julia followed Tom and the others to the file cabinets

that lined one wall and he showed them where to start. She took a small stack of case files and went back to her brand-new desk, *Detective Julia Taylor* freshly engraved on her nameplate. Yep, this was her life now, her name, her identity.

She could get used to it.

2
EMERY

"Please don't..."

Emery Ellison's life – and career – flashed before her eyes as she watched a fifth grader make a screaming leap at a low-hanging grapevine.

In her mind, the thick but dry vine was about to snap under the kid's weight, but not until the apex of his swing. He'd go flying, crash down on one of the many jagged shale boulders on the trail, and crack his head wide open.

There'd be blood everywhere...

Crying children...

She'd lose her job...

Her warning had been soft and tentative. Who knew if the kid even heard her, or if he just saw her for what she was – a grown-up with very little authority over him who could easily be ignored.

In any case, he was swinging around like freaking Tarzan now, and she was just waiting for that vine to snap, making more ineffective suggestions like, "Excuse me, can you please get down…"

"Mason, get down from there this second!"

His teacher finally noticed what he was doing and the tone of her voice was enough to give Emery the impulse to freeze and apologize. It did the trick – Mason immediately dropped back down to the ground, safely on his feet again.

The teacher – Mrs. Cardone – scowled at Mason until he was sufficiently psychically beaten, then turned to Emery.

"I'm so sorry, Miss Ellison," she said. "We talked about listening to adults before we left school today." She leaned a little closer and said under her breath, "You really gotta work on your 'hey, you little shit' tone. It's the only thing some of them respond to."

"Noted, thanks."

Emery worked for a university, primarily doing research, so her surprise was justified when her job duties expanded to leading field trips for kids of all age ranges and all over Fox County. She'd take them into the woods around the university and teach them about the mushrooms and other fungi that grew there.

It was a community outreach program designed to raise the university's profile and get kids interested in science. And when the previous community outreach liaison retired, Emery's boss had promised her that this arrangement would be temporary.

He also promised it'd get easier the more practice she had.

It'd been a full school year and she'd led about half a dozen field trips, and she was no closer to learning how to control a rowdy bunch of kids who were so excited that it was finally warm enough to go outside again that all they wanted to do was run roughshod over the forest. Emery worried constantly – in equal parts about them injuring themselves and injuring the delicate ecosystem they were so hell-bent on trampling.

And her 'hey, you little shit' voice was admittedly not good.

There was *one* thing she was pretty damn good at when it came to these field trips, though. And she quite enjoyed it, too.

"Everyone, can I get your attention?"

Not a single child looked at her.

Mrs. Cardone took pity. She whistled through her fingers and shouted loud enough to make Emery wince, "Listen up!"

Now, two dozen sets of eyes were on Emery, and she had to take advantage of their attention while she had it. She'd been leading them around the forest for about twenty minutes now, and she'd finally found what she'd been hoping for.

"Have any of you heard of the destroying angel?" she asked, and saw the expressions in all their eyes change. Obedient attention became genuine intrigue as she listed off a few more nicknames. "Death cap. The fool's mushroom. *Amanita bisporigera*. The most toxic genus of mushroom in the world... and it grows right here in Pennsylvania."

She pointed to a couple of large white mushrooms poking out of the rotting leaves on the forest floor, about ten feet off the trail. She'd been keeping her eye out for them the whole hike, and at this time of year, it was pretty much guaranteed they'd spot at least one.

"Come closer, let's take a look," she said.

The kids looked at her like she was inviting them to stick their arms in a tiger cage. She shouldn't enjoy it as much as she did, but it was nice to get a little respect from a group of ten-year-olds that had been giving her hell all morning. Especially Mason, whose eyes were wide with intrigue.

"It's safe," she promised, waving them on as she approached the mushrooms. "You don't want to touch them without thoroughly washing your hands after, and you never, *never* want to eat one. But you can look."

Mrs. Cardone stayed on the trail while the kids tentatively approached Emery. She crouched down and they all followed her lead, gathering around while she taught them how to identify and steer clear of destroying angels.

She may have gone a little heavy on the description of what happens if you *do* eat one – payback's a bitch, Mason. But one thing was for sure – none of these kids, no one who'd ever taken a lesson from Emery Ellison on mushroom identification, would make the mistake of eating one of these.

3
JULIA

The stack of open cases on Julia's desk was ever so slightly shorter by the end of the day. She'd read through two of them as thoroughly as she could and decided that there were no loose ends or unfollowed leads, so they'd have to go back in the file cabinet again.

Most cold cases didn't get resolved unless new evidence came to light on its own – like when technological advances allowed DNA to be identified where it hadn't previously been possible, or when the perp committed a new crime and ended up being tied to old ones as well.

Just looking through files, hoping for something to jump out at you, was generally a fool's errand, but it was part of the job – especially when there was nothing else to do. And on her first day on duty at Fox County PD, it appeared there was nothing else to do but due diligence.

She'd gotten to know the other new hires a bit better during lunch. The five of them had been doing onboarding together for a week, but a lot of their training had been remote learning modules so they hadn't gotten to talk in person much until now. Today, they went down the street to a diner Arlen recommended when she and Renee got back from their investigation.

They had sandwiches and got to know each other. There was Tate Macawi, a transfer from small-town South Dakota looking for a city with a bit more action where she could prove herself. "I'm here to climb the ladder," she said, completely unafraid to state her intentions. "I'm aiming for chief someday."

"Here?" Julia asked.

"Wherever I can get the job," she said.

"Well, I'll just be happy to be a good homicide detective," Ariel Sterner answered. She was local and had been recently promoted from patrol, which was the same story as Lena Wolf, the fourth member of their new team.

And then there was Renee Duvall.

An experienced detective like Julia and Tate, she'd transferred from the missing persons department into homicide. And she'd taken an immediate dislike to Julia for no reason Julia could determine.

The feeling was now mutual.

"I haven't decided where I ultimately want to end up," Renee said. "Missing persons was interesting for a while. Homicide ought to be a challenge. I like to keep pushing myself."

"You don't want to settle down?" Julia asked.

Renee's eyes bore into her. "Seems like you know

something about that. You left Grand Rapids pretty quick, didn't you?"

The table went silent for a few beats as heat rushed into Julia's cheeks and she tried to think of an answer. The whole reason she left Michigan was so that she *wouldn't* have to talk about her past. The last thing she wanted to do was invite it to follow her here.

Then thankfully, Tate announced, "Looks like our lunch hour's almost up. Ready to head back?" and the conversation moved on.

In the afternoon, they all kept reviewing cold cases and learned a little more about their two superiors, Tom Logan and Arlen Rose. Tom was a man of few words, serious, focused on his work and pretty resistant to the attempts Julia and the other new hires made to draw him out.

Arlen was chattier and more open, and Tom was friendly with her, at least. By the end of the day everyone knew that Arlen desperately wanted to propose to her girlfriend, who worked at the medical examiner's office, but she was also determined to get it right. This meant that even though Arlen decided to propose three months ago, she still hadn't popped the question.

"Do you think you've changed your mind so many times because you're nervous she might say no?" Tom asked.

Julia was doing her best to appear to be working rather than listening. Renee was making no such attempt.

"How long have you been dating?" she asked.

"About a year and a half," Arlen said, then turned

back to Tom. "I don't think she'll say no... I just want it to be perfect. You only get one shot to make that memory, you know?"

"Ideally," Tom grunted. His desk phone rang and he answered it with a gruff, "Logan." Julia perked up, no longer pretending not to listen. She was on deck, after all. When Tom hung up, he looked at her. "We just got a call."

Tate looked at the clock on the wall – now just fifteen minutes til the end of the shift. "Overtime on your first day – lucky duck."

"Come on," Tom said, grabbing the FCPD-logoed jacket slung over the back of his chair and not waiting for Julia to catch up as he headed for the elevator.

Most of the employees around here took the stairs – the building was only three floors – but Tom walked with a subtle limp. Julia knew from some gossip Renee shared at lunch that he'd been involved in a shooting a few years ago, though Renee hadn't provided the nitty-gritty details. Not that Julia was in a position to pry into people's backgrounds.

She hopped on the elevator with Tom just as the doors were sliding closed. "Where we going?"

"Hospital," he said. "Acute liver failure on an otherwise healthy twenty-five-year-old."

"Very unusual." Her mind was already whirring with the limited medical knowledge she had about liver failure. Acute, that meant it was a recent development, and healthy twenty-somethings didn't generally have livers that just quit working on their own. "Dispatch say anything else?"

"Nope," Tom said. Man of few words indeed – Julia tried not to take it personally.

They went down to the parking deck and got in Tom's behemoth of an unmarked SUV. He drove them to Fox County Hospital and found their decedent in a private room in the intensive care unit.

"Take notes," Tom said at the threshold of the room. "I know you got three years under your belt in Michigan, but I don't know you from Adam so you gotta prove yourself just like everybody else at FCPD. You're second on this case til I say otherwise, got it?"

Julia swallowed her annoyance. She had a long list of commendations and achievements from her time in Grand Rapids, but she'd been forced to leave her entire history behind in order to get the anonymity she needed. No one on her new team knew what her career was like. To them, she might as well be fresh out of the academy.

She pulled out her notebook and followed Tom into the room.

The decedent was lying in the hospital bed, a white sheet pulled up over his head. There was an investigator from the medical examiner's office in the room, unfolding a black body bag in preparation to move the body, and she smiled when she saw Tom.

"Oh good, you gonna help me do the transfer so I don't have to flag down a nurse?"

"Not with my bum leg, Ross," Tom said.

The investigator, a fit brunette with a tan complexion, rolled her eyes. "Why is it that injury always gets more severe whenever you're trying to weasel out of something?"

"It doesn't," Tom objected. "Taylor, you wanna jump in?"

"Move the body?" Julia asked. "Yeah, I guess so."

It was nothing she hadn't done before, although she'd yet to find anyone for whom it was their favorite part of the job. Especially after the body went stiff.

"Newbie?" Ross asked as Julia set down her notebook.

"At Fox County, yes," she answered. "Three years on the force though."

"Maya Ross. Nice to meet ya."

Julia's brows rose as she recognized the name – this had to be the Maya who was Arlen's girlfriend, soon to be fiancée. Julia quickly wiped the recognition off her face and introduced herself, then got into position on the other side of the hospital bed.

"So what do we know?" Tom asked while Maya laid out the body bag on a gurney.

"Not a whole lot yet," she said. "Decedent is Brandon Hawthorne, twenty-five years old, been in the ICU for three days. Mom found him on death's door and brought him to the ER. He was at the very top of the liver transplant list but it didn't do him any good."

Maya pulled the hospital sheet off the body. Julia noticed the man's hands and feet had already been covered in paper bags to preserve any potential evidence of foul play. He was wearing a hospital gown and his skin was alarmingly jaundiced.

Julia and Maya maneuvered the body from bed to gurney and into the black bag, then Maya said, "I'm done here – not much for me to see in the ICU. Doc said she'd be back in a few, she was going to check on the toxicology labs they ordered while they were treating him. She suspects poison of some kind – that's why I called you."

Tom grunted – one of his standard responses, Julia was learning – and Maya unlocked the wheels of the gurney and started pushing it toward the door.

"Do you want help?" Julia asked.

"Nah," Maya said. "Done this a million times. I'll call you when the autopsy's scheduled."

"Thanks," Tom said.

Julia looked around for a paper chart like some of the smaller hospitals back home had, but Fox County appeared to be fully electronic. So she followed Tom as he waved her back into the hallway. They went to the nurse's station and he asked about the decedent's family.

"They still here?"

The nurse on duty nodded. "His parents are in the private waiting room. Would you like me to take you to them?"

"Please," Tom said.

They walked down the hall, past a number of patient rooms full of beeping monitors, to a room with a closed door that had an oblong window in it. A woman with gray-streaked hair and a thickly bearded man sat together on a sofa, and when the nurse opened the door, the sound of the woman's cries echoed down the hallway.

"Mr. and Mrs. Hawthorne?" the nurse announced himself. "The doctor will be back with the lab results shortly. In the meantime, there are a couple police officers who'd like to speak with you."

The woman's eyes reddened as she struggled to hold back her tears, and the man nodded, his voice thick as he said, "Okay."

Tom stepped into the room and the nurse held the door for Julia. She took a steadying breath before entering, and the nurse left them, the door closing softly. Tom held out his hand to them both.

"I'm Detective Logan and this is Detective Taylor," he said. "We're very sorry for your loss."

"I can't even process it," Mr. Hawthorne said. "It happened so fast."

"Would it be all right if we ask you a few questions?" Tom asked, taking a seat in a chair across from the sofa. "I promise we'll be brief."

Mrs. Hawthorne swiped at her wet cheeks and Julia found a box of tissues on a nearby table, offering them to her. "If it will help us find out what happened to Brandon. The doctor told us she suspected poison!"

"I heard you were the one who found Brandon," Tom said, his tone surprisingly gentle. "Can you tell me more about that? Did he live with you?"

"No," Mrs. Hawthorne said. "He had an apartment, but he kept in contact with us pretty often, mostly texts.

That's why I got worried and went over there when I hadn't heard from him."

"In how long?" Tom prompted.

"Over a week," she answered, then choked up. Julia passed her another tissue, Mrs. Hawthorne took it, and then buried her face in her husband's sweater, mumbling her words. "It was so awful."

"I was home raking leaves when she went to check on him," Mr. Hawthorne took over. "I thought she was hovering – he's a twenty-five-year-old man, after all, is it that weird if he doesn't talk to his parents in a couple days?"

"It was weird *for him*," Mrs. Hawthorne said, face still buried.

"He lived alone?" Tom asked.

"Yes," Mr. Hawthorne answered. "He had a lot of friends though, and they came and went all the time – at the apartment, and at our house before that."

"Girlfriend? Partner?" Julia asked.

"Yes," Mr. Hawthorne said. "Amanda. They'd been dating what, four months, honey?"

Mrs. Hawthorne lifted her head, mascara smeared all over her eyelids. "Yes. She came to visit yesterday but he wasn't conscious. She's been texting him all day today – we've got his phone. I can't bring myself to answer, to tell her what happened."

"We can inform her if you'd like," Tom said. "And I'm sorry, but we'll need to collect the phone. It might help us figure out what happened to your son."

She frowned, but pulled a smartphone out of the

handbag sitting on the floor at her feet, handing it over. "We'll get it back, right?"

"Yes, after the investigation."

That word set her off again and she grabbed another tissue.

"Does it have a passcode?" Tom asked.

"His birthday," Mr. Hawthorne said, then provided the number.

Tom unlocked the phone just to be sure it worked, scrolled through the messages and asked, "Amanda Drake?"

"That's her," Mr. Hawthorne said.

Tom handed the phone to Julia, who tried to be discreet about wrapping it in a tissue to preserve any trace evidence that might be on it, however unlikely.

"Do you know your son's whereabouts in the days before you found him in his apartment?" Tom asked. "Anyone he might have seen, anywhere he might have gone – especially any food he may have eaten and with whom?"

Both of the Hawthornes shook their heads. "We couldn't reach him," Mrs. Hawthorne said. "We just don't know!"

Tom waited, silence being a valuable tool in the investigative toolbox. It made people consider their answers, filling in any details they may have omitted the first time around.

"He probably went hiking with his friend, Nick," Mr. Hawthorne said. "They go all the time, at least once a week, barely ever skip it even in the winter."

"You know Nick's last name?" Tom asked.

"Wilkins, they've been friends since elementary school."

Tom looked to Julia, who wrote the name down. They'd have to check the phone for a Nick Wilkins later and track him down, along with the girlfriend.

There was a soft knock at the door, and then it opened and a pretty older woman with cat-eye glasses stepped in. She noticed Tom and Julia's presence and said, "I'm Dr. Nasir, is this a good time?"

Tom showed the doctor his badge, but deferred to the Hawthornes, who said it was fine if they stayed.

Dr. Nasir held up a tablet. "I've just come from the lab. Brandon's toxicology results are in and it's what we were afraid of – amatoxin."

"So he was poisoned?" Mrs. Hawthorne asked, her voice watery again.

"We still don't know the source, since Brandon wasn't able to tell us himself," Dr. Nasir reminded her. "You told us that he often hikes in the woods, so it's possible this was accidental. Perhaps he ate something on the trail thinking it was something else."

"Brandon wouldn't have eaten a poison mushroom," Mr. Hawthorne argued. "He was smarter than that!"

"We hiked with him lots of times," Mrs. Hawthorne added. "He wasn't eating things he found along the way like some animal trying to survive the winter!"

"If someone poisoned your son, we'll figure it out," Tom promised.

"I have to tend to other patients, I just wanted to let

you know the lab results," Dr. Nasir said. "Please, take as much time as you need here, and let me know if there's anything I can do."

"Bring him back," Mrs. Hawthorne said, and Mr. Hawthorne cupped his hand over her head, drawing her down to his shoulder.

"We'll leave you for now too," Tom said, standing and extending his business card to Mr. Hawthorne. "We'll need you to come down to the station and talk with us in a couple of days, okay?"

They nodded, clearly in shock, and Tom ushered Julia into the hallway after the doctor. The three of them went back to the nurse's station where they'd be well out of earshot of the Hawthornes, and Tom asked, "So, what do you think, doc? Accidental or foul play?"

"There's also the possibility of suicide," Julia added, although from the picture the Hawthornes had painted, it didn't sound like their son was suicidal.

"The vast majority of amatoxin deaths are accidental," Dr. Nasir said. "Not that I have personal experience – they're also pretty rare. If it was more common, maybe we would have figured out what was going on with him sooner and we could have started him on a more targeted therapy."

"Could he have survived it?" Julia asked.

"Yes, with early enough intervention," the doctor said. "But the poison had been in his system at least a week by the time he came into the ER and got admitted to the ICU. He was already in acute liver failure, and his kidneys were going by then too."

"So what, he just sat around his apartment for a week while his organs shut down?" Tom wondered. "Who would do that?"

"And why," Julia added. Again, the question of how much Brandon Hawthorne wanted to live surfaced in her mind.

In any case, her first shift as an FCPD detective just got a whole lot more interesting.

4
EMERY

"Are you fucking kidding me?"

Emery pushed away from her desk, her chair spinning of its own accord.

"What?"

The voice was unexpected and she jumped, turning back toward the door to her office. Luckily, it was her best work friend – well, best friend period – Monica. If it had been her boss, he certainly would have had something to say about the f-bomb.

"Come in," Emery waved. Monica shut the door behind her and plopped down in the chair across from Emery's desk. "Remember that kid from the field trip yesterday who thought he was Tarzan?"

Monica rolled her eyes. "You only mentioned him half a dozen times."

"He was ripping the forest apart!"

Monica laughed. "He swung on a grapevine. They're invasive, and it was probably dead anyway."

"He was a menace," Emery insisted. "And so is his mother."

She turned her computer monitor toward Monica, who squinted as she read the email that Tarzan's mother had just sent complaining about how Emery had traumatized him with her cautionary tale about killer mushrooms.

"Ugh, she CC'd Glen," Monica noticed.

"Of course she did."

Glen was their boss, the head of the university's mycology department, a tenured dinosaur with zero sense of humor. And even though he'd been the one to saddle Emery with the community outreach duties and seemed to be in no hurry to hire a new faculty member, he had no problem endlessly criticizing her performance.

"Hey, maybe this will be the thing that finally gets him off his butt to fill that position," Monica said cheerily.

She was faculty too, but unlike Emery, she taught more than she researched – which was probably what had saved her from doing community outreach.

"Don't get me wrong, I would *love* to get back to my research full-time," Emery said. There was a half-written paper on the ideal growth conditions of mycelium in Pennsylvania on her hard drive, but who knew when she'd have time to finish it at this rate. "But if I get pulled off community outreach because of this kid's mom…"

She let out a huff and pushed off the edge of her desk, sending her chair swirling with a frustrated flourish.

"I get it," Monica said. "You don't wanna get fired."

"Don't even say that word." Emery shuddered.

"How about another f-word?" Emery's eyes widened and Monica laughed. "Food, have you heard of it?"

Emery's stomach rumbled, reminding her it had been a while since she stuffed a protein bar into her cheeks on the drive to campus this morning. "Rings a faint bell."

"Come on," Monica said, holding out her hand and pulling Emery out of her chair. "Tarzan's mom – and Glen – can wait til after we split a pizza in the student union."

Emery laughed. "You may be eating for two right now, but I can't afford to. You get the pizza, I'll have a salad."

"You always get salad," Monica griped, hand going instinctively to her belly.

She'd announced a couple months ago that she was pregnant, very considerately planning her family around the university's semester system. Glen had been pleased with that, but Emery couldn't decide how she felt about the fact that Monica was already calling her an honorary aunt. She never knew what to do with kids, and sometimes she didn't fare any better with adults.

"Whatever, I could totally crush a whole pizza without your help today," Monica said, practically dragging her out the door.

The student union wasn't particularly crowded – they were there in between the lunch rush and the afternoon snacking rush. Emery picked at her salad, her mind still mostly on that nasty email waiting for her back in her office, and Monica did indeed 'crush' a personal pan pizza and then got ice cream out of the soft-serve machine.

"You sure you don't want some?" she asked, trying to tempt Emery into indulging as she filled up a cone. "You're stick-thin, girl."

"I'm fit," Emery corrected. She was tall, five-foot-nine in flats, and she'd retained the long, lean body that had come from years of cross-country running, first in high school, then college. Besides, she just didn't have much of a sweet tooth – something Monica considered weird even before her pregnancy.

After Monica's dessert, they headed back across campus to the science buildings all clustered together, and Emery could hear her office phone ringing from all the way down the hall.

"Shit, I hope that's not Glen," she muttered as she made a dash for her office.

"He'd just drop in," Monica called after her, which only made Emery feel mildly better.

"Hello?" She was a little frazzled when she lifted the receiver to her lips, quickly composing herself. "This is Dr. Ellison."

"Hi," a warm, somewhat uncertain-sounding female voice said. "I'm Julia Taylor." Strange, she seemed to trip over her own name. "I work for Fox County PD and we need a mycologist. I was told you consulted for us once before."

"I did," Emery confirmed, stepping around her desk to sit down and grab a notepad. "How can I help?"

The last case she worked on had involved providing

expert testimony in court regarding black mold in an apartment building, attempting to prove the landlord's negligence. It'd been fascinating and by far the best part of her new community outreach duties.

Reason one: adults.

Reason two: like just about everyone else on the planet, she was a *CSI* fan and consulting on cases was a lot of fun. Monica, an even bigger crime drama junkie, had been unendingly jealous.

And reason three... FCPD just happened to have a *lot* of gorgeous queer women on staff. Even if most of them were taken, Emery was not above enjoying the eye candy while she worked on the case.

"I'm investigating a death by amatoxin," Julia Taylor said.

Emery nearly dropped the receiver. Even though just yesterday she'd just been scaring little kids with the dangers of Amanitas, there were only one or two deaths per year from them in the entire country. What were the odds?

"The toxicologist over at the medical examiner's office will need an antigen sample so she can test the decedent for the presence of the toxin," Julia went on.

"Sure, we've got that on hand, I can drop it off in the morning," Emery said.

"And there's one more thing," Julia said. "I just got done speaking to a friend of decedent, who says the two of them went hiking a couple of weeks ago and saw some peculiar mushrooms. He swears they didn't pick any, but said that a few looked like they'd already been picked. He took a photo."

"Can you email it to me?"

"Sure, what's your address?"

Emery gave it, then swiveled to her computer to wait for the photo to come through. Meanwhile, Julia kept talking.

"Can you make an ID from a photo?"

"Not a definitive one," Emery said. "I'll need to see them in person, and do a microscopic exam in the lab to be sure."

"The friend thinks he can guide us back to the general area," Julia said. "Are you available to come help us look and make the ID?"

"When?"

"Tomorrow?"

Emery looked at her desk calendar. She didn't have any meetings planned, and it would have been a good day to work on her research. But the less time she spent in her office, the less chance Glen would have to get on her case about the email from Tarzan's mom.

"Morning is best for spotting mushrooms," she said. "Tell me which trailhead and I'll meet you there about nine."

"Wonderful," Julia said, and Emery could hear her smile in her tone. "I'll send the photo now, along with the rest of the case file."

"I'll take a look," Emery promised.

Was this woman one of the gorgeous ones?

Better yet, was she available?

5
JULIA

The morning air was brisk, and Julia hadn't gotten her department-issued jacket yet. Instead, she stood in a crisp cotton button-up, her sidearm tucked into her customary shoulder holster beneath a blazer that wasn't at all appropriate for a hike. She had her arms crossed over her chest, and her borrowed black FCPD sedan was breaking some of the wind at her back.

Beside her, Brandon Hawthorne's hiking buddy, Nick Wilkins, was talking a mile a minute, oblivious to the cold. "...so I took a picture because I'd never seen anything like it before – neither had Brandon. I mean, these don't look too poisonous to me, but I guess what do I know, right? And I definitely didn't see him eat any – he wasn't *that* kind of outdoorsy. Jesus... *wasn't*. I still can't believe he's dead, I keep waiting for it all to be some big, sick joke..."

He hadn't stopped talking since he showed up at the

station this morning to meet Julia. She was flying solo today because Tom had gotten a lead on new evidence in a case he started working last month. It would have been nicer if she got to take charge of the Hawthorne case because her new boss believed in her and not because he had no other choice, but she'd take what she could get.

And what she had was a nervously chatty hipster.

Nick was in his mid-twenties, just like Brandon, and so far he'd been entirely forthcoming and helpful. Julia didn't view him as a suspect in spite of his obvious nervousness, but you never ruled anyone completely out until the case was solved.

"...can't even imagine what Amanda must be feeling right now," he was saying. "I mean, I loved the guy, but we were just friends..."

A hunter-green hybrid coupe pulled into the gravel lot and parked next to the unmarked, and Julia sent up a silent thanks to the universe. Nick was just blabbering on because it was his way of coping, but still – she wouldn't mind some reinforcements.

"Is this the... what did you call them? Mixologist?"

Julia stifled a laugh. "Mycologist," she said. "Scientist who studies mushrooms. And yes, I assume this is her."

The driver door popped open and a woman stepped out of the car. She had tawny brown skin and long, lean legs with muscled calves peeking out above a pair of hiking boots. She was in utilitarian cargo shorts and a soft-looking pullover sweater, and the dimples on her cheeks were so deep they showed even when she wasn't smiling.

When her carob-brown eyes met Julia's, she did smile, and the overall effect was that of a drop-dead-gorgeous nerd. Especially when she reached back into the car and produced a fanny pack.

"Are you Julia?"

Julia cleared her throat and held out her hand. "Detective Taylor. Nice to meet you."

"Dr. Emery Ellison," she answered, those dimples deepening as a spark ignited in her eyes. Then she looked to Julia's chatty companion. "You must be the hiking buddy. I'm so sorry for your loss."

Nick nodded, introduced himself, and held his phone up for Emery to see a few more photos he'd taken, all without pausing for breath. "Like I was telling the detective, I can't remember exactly where this is, but it's on the trail somewhere, so hopefully there's enough in these pictures for you to go on. The mushrooms, they were so weird, a perfect circle like somebody came out there and planted them that way. Well, except the ones that were missing."

Emery didn't seem as overwhelmed by the guy as Julia had been. She took his phone and examined the pictures, nodding in response.

"This is called a fairy ring," she explained. "They're actually not uncommon, and there's a lot of lore surrounding them." She glanced to Julia with a smile. "No pun intended."

"Are they dangerous?" the detective asked.

"Their existence? No," Emery said. She looked a bit older than Julia, maybe a decade, and her dimples became pronounced whenever she spoke. "They just mean that there's fungal growth present beneath the surface of the ground. They can be made up of a variety of different mushroom species, though, and some of those are dangerous."

"Can you tell if these are the kind that can kill somebody?" Nick asked.

"Not from a photo," she said, handing back his phone. "Shall we set off?"

"Yep, I'll let you take the lead on this – not exactly my area of expertise," Julia said, sweeping her arm in the direction of the trailhead.

"Well, that's what you've got me for," Emery said. She stopped just shy of winking, and Julia felt warmth building in her cheeks. Damn, was this hot mycologist really giving her looks?

Seriously, how could someone currently clipping on a *fanny pack* be so hot? It was criminal... and perhaps Julia would have to make an arrest.

She briefly allowed herself to fantasize about clicking her cuffs around Emery's wrists, then forced herself to stop. She'd been worrying since the day she applied for this job that it would end spectacularly badly, and she was in no position to get flirty with *anyone,* let alone someone she was working with.

Julia followed the two of them up the trail. It was a path of loose gravel about three feet wide and winding into the woods. There were a lot of these trails all over the county, or so Tom told her, available to the public and well-utilized.

So far, there was absolutely nothing out of the ordinary, and after about a hundred feet, the loose gravel yielded to rougher terrain – bare dirt with rocks embedded in the soil here and there.

"How far out did you see the fairy ring?" Emery asked Nick.

"I don't really know," he said. "Maybe a mile? The whole trail is three miles."

They mostly walked in silence – Nick in front, looking for anything familiar that would help him locate the mushrooms in question. Emery next, concentrating hard and sweeping her gaze back and forth on both sides of the trail, looking for anything of interest.

And Julia bringing up the rear, looking everywhere but at Emery's perfectly sculpted backside.

She didn't know a shitake from a pile of... bear poo. If there *were* bears in this area. Michigan had them, and she'd once been called out on the death scene of a man foolish enough to attempt to keep one as a pet. Didn't work out any better for him than Julia's last relationship had for her.

She was just starting to go down a metaphorical rabbit hole, ruminating on her life back in Michigan, when the toe of her boot caught on a large rock in the trail.

"Oh fuck!"

It was all she had time to say before she was sprawling forward, arms out, prepared to feel the exquisite burn of skinned knees and scraped palms that she hadn't experienced since she was a kid.

Emery whirled around, lightning-fast, and put out her arms to catch her. And instead of sharp rocks, Julia's palms filled with soft, surprisingly full breasts.

Yeah, she'd just full-on groped the scientist consulting on her first Fox County case.

Horror and embarrassment washed over her in equal measure and she found her footing as fast as she could, yanking her hands back like Emery's chest was a hot stovetop.

"Are you okay?"

"I am so sorry!"

"It's fine," Emery said, both of them breathless and flustered. "Are you hurt?"

"No, you, uh... broke my fall." God, could the earth just open up and swallow her right now? Because that was the only way Julia could imagine escaping this moment. "Thanks?"

"You're... welcome," Emery said.

Julia hazarded a look into her eyes just long enough to see mirth in them. Was Emery merely enjoying her humiliation, or had she actually liked Julia's hands on her too?

The best thing – the only thing – was to just forget that it happened.

"Should we keep going?"

"After you," Emery said, holding out her hand so that Julia could pass her and take up the middle spot in their little caravan. So, she definitely wasn't offering her chest for fall-breaking purposes again.

Another wave of embarrassment flooded Julia's

cheeks as she stepped past Emery, and then she saw the amusement written all over Nick's face. He'd clearly seen the whole incident, and now she was thinking she might have to resort to homicide to make sure her embarrassment didn't make it out of the woods.

She was a detective, after all… she knew how to get away with it.

6
EMERY

She felt Julia's hands on her breasts long after they'd left.

She really should have been fully focused on mushroom hunting. A death investigation hung in the balance, and yet, she couldn't stop thinking about how adorably flustered the detective had gotten. It was an innocent mistake – an embarrassing one, of course – but Julia had reacted like the sexual harassment police were going to pop out of the trees and arrest her on the spot.

It was cute... as was Detective Taylor.

If anyone was going to cop a feel five minutes after meeting her, Emery didn't mind that it had been Julia.

Concentrate, she told herself as they walked along.

It was sunny, the day warming up quickly, and there weren't any other hikers so far – not in the morning on a weekday. But Emery wasn't out here to enjoy a stroll and fixate on how Julia's hands had felt on her.

She kept her head on a swivel, sweeping her eyes over

the most likely places for mushrooms to pop up on both sides of the trail – and also periodically glancing at the trail ahead, keeping an eye on Julia's footing in case she tripped again. Emery figured she'd be more comfortable walking in front of her after that, and if she turned out to be accident-prone, then sandwiched between two people she'd be less likely to twist an ankle and need to be carried back to the parking lot.

"Can I help?" Julia asked a few minutes after they resumed their walk. "Just tell me what I'm looking for."

"Basically, big white mushrooms," Emery told her. "There are a few varieties in the *Amanita* genus, and they do look pretty similar but I took a look at your decedent's lab results last night–"

"Decedent?" Nick asked from the front of the line.

Emery cringed. She hadn't actually interacted with the family members of the deceased last time she worked with the police. Tact was not her strong suit – just ask Tarzan's mom – and here was yet another example.

"I'm sorry. It's a technical term."

"His name was Brandon," Nick answered.

"Yes, I know," Emery said. "Again, I am sorry." When he didn't speak again, she continued her thought. "Brandon's lab results showed he ingested *Amanita bisporigera*. Immature, it will appear small, white and rounded, somewhat similar to a grocery store button mushroom. As they mature, they grow taller and their caps flatten out."

Julia looked around for a moment. "So, big white mushroom, got it."

"Or little white mushroom," Emery said with a smile.

And then she couldn't help herself. She added, "But perhaps you should just keep an eye out for rocks on the trail."

Julia turned around, a glimmer in her gaze. Her voice was a whisper when she asked, "You don't want to catch me again?"

And then before Emery could answer, Julia whipped her head back around, her long, dark ponytail nearly smacking Emery in the face. She got a whiff of Julia's scent – the warm comfort of sandalwood.

And then Nick asked, "What's that?"

Emery looked where he was pointing, a dozen yards off the trail where a small creek ran through the forest. Erosion had taken its toll, carving away the side of a hill leading down to the creek, and it left a few trees sitting somewhat precariously, their roots exposed. Emery saw no evidence of fungal growth.

"I don't see anything."

"There," he insisted, pointing to the base of one of the trees. "What *is* that?"

Emery squinted, and stepped off the trail for a closer look. Maybe she needed to change her contact prescription because she didn't...

"Oh, there," she said, catching a little hint of something white. "Good eye."

It was really tangled up in the roots – probably not fungal – but now her interest was piqued. She picked her way across last year's fallen leaves and through thorny underbrush, Julia and Nick both following her.

"Stay here," Julia instructed him when they got to the creek bed.

"You coming?" Emery asked.

Julia nodded, and Emery held out her hand. She wasn't sure if Julia would take it – if she'd be too proud after her fall, or if she'd see it as a sign of weakness. Even with the small amount of experience Emery had with detectives, she knew they could be a stubborn bunch.

But Julia took her hand, allowing Emery to steady her as she picked her way across two flat, wet stones and onto the opposite shore.

"Thanks," she said before releasing her.

Emery nodded, and somewhere in the back of her mind – nowhere near the top of her priority list – she noticed that Nick had disobeyed Julia, joining them on this side of the creek.

But now that he was here, he suddenly acted like he didn't want to be. "Oh God, is that what I think it is?"

Emery was allowing herself to get *far* too distracted by Julia's big brown eyes and the perfect Cupid's bow of her lips. She'd practically forgotten there was a reason they were going off-trail.

She turned her attention to the tree roots and a gasp escaped from her lips.

"Oh fuck," Julia said for the second time that morning.

And behind them, there was the sound of Nick retching into the stream.

Tangled in the tree roots, peeking out here and there, were human skeletal remains. And how did Emery, humble lab-bound mycologist, know that they were human? Because the cranium was the white bit Nick had spotted from the trail. A thick root grew out from one eye socket, so big now that it was starting to form itself around the skull.

7
JULIA

"How the hell does that even happen?" Nick asked after he finished emptying his stomach.

"Tree roots are kind of like honey badgers," Julia said distractedly.

Nick was still looking sort of green and he just gave her a confused look, but Emery knew just what she meant and filled in the rest of the quote. "They don't give a shit."

He still looked unamused, so Julia gave him her first-impression thoughts, while also gently guiding him and Emery back across the stream and away from the remains. "The person could have died many years ago, before the tree was even there. Maybe they were buried in that spot and the tree grew over them, or the tree was there and the roots grew into the gravesite."

"Could there be more?" Nick looked like he was

going to crawl out of his skin, like he'd accidentally stumbled into an *Evil Dead* remake.

Julia didn't want to freak him out even further so she didn't tell him that yes, it was entirely possible that there could be more bodies – this area had a long history of habitation as far back as the Stone Age.

Then again, the tree's trunk was only about ten inches wide so it *probably* hadn't seen the turn of any centuries.

Julia informed them that the hike would have to be postponed while she secured the area and got the coroner out here. Internally, she was kind of geeking out – it wasn't every day you found skeletal remains being swallowed up by a tree. Could she ask Tom to let her switch cases? Would he frown on that request, considering how nonexistent her seniority was?

She took out her phone and called dispatch, who said they'd send an investigator from the medical examiner's office.

"We're about twenty minutes down the trail," Julia told the dispatcher. "Maybe half a mile?"

She looked to Nick, who nodded. "I recognize the stream. We're not far from where Brandon and I saw the... what was it called?"

"Fairy ring," Emery filled in.

"Do you want me to hike back out to the parking lot to meet the ME?" Julia asked the dispatcher.

"Let me ask."

There was a brief silence on the line, during which

Julia stole a look at Emery. She didn't seem nearly as shaken as Nick – in fact, she was bending down, trying to get a better look at how the tree roots had tangled themselves around the skeleton. Curiosity was always a good quality in a woman...

"Hello?" the dispatcher said into Julia's ear.

"I'm here."

"Investigator says she's familiar with the trail, you can wait with the body and she'll come to you."

"Great, how long?"

"About half an hour."

Julia hung up, and relayed the information to her hiking buddies, concluding with, "So I guess maybe you two should head home and we can try to find the fairy ring another day? Maybe tomorrow? I have to stay here and secure the scene."

Emery frowned. "I have a pretty full week ahead of me."

"And I'm not sure I ever want to set foot on this trail again, now that I know it's a crime scene," Nick said, grimacing.

"Well, it's not *definitely* a crime," Julia pointed out. "Like I said, it could just be a very old gravesite."

"Either way... 'the woods are full of skeletons' is the start of a horror movie," he answered.

"What if Nick and I hike ahead, find the fairy ring, and then circle back to see how you're doing here?" Emery suggested.

Nick did not look enthusiastic about the idea of

circling back, but it was the best compromise Julia could think of. "Yeah, that should work. Thank you."

"Anything special I need to do when we find them?" Emery asked.

"Take pictures," Julia said. "And use your phone to get the exact coordinates of the mushrooms, in case we need to go back later for a more thorough investigation. Oh, and disturb the scene as little as possible…"

Damn, the more she listed, the more things she thought of – there was a reason she was on this hike too. She waved Emery closer, and enjoyed the way her tight curls bounced around her temples as she moved.

Julia leaned in – close enough to feel the warmth of Emery's body, and the freshness of her scent. "Don't let Nick step off the trail once you find it. I don't think the kid had anything to do with his friend's death, but I can't have him contaminating the scene just in case."

If Tom was here, he'd have something to say about this choice but if this was the only day she had an expert mycologist at her disposal, she'd have to make do. Besides, if Tom was here, they could split up and the problem would be solved.

Emery stayed close, their faces only inches apart, as she met Julia's gaze. "Are you sending me into the forest with a potential murderer, detective?"

"I trust that you can handle yourself," Julia said. She knew Emery was teasing, but at the same time, she was making her question every choice she was making.

But Emery winked at her, then hopped back across the creek and climbed up the bank with Nick. They disappeared up the trail, and Julia stood there with her hands on her hips, the morning sun starting to bake down on her, a skeleton beneath the tree at her back.

Yeah, this was a strange life, but it was the one she'd chosen and she loved it.

8
EMERY

They didn't have to go far to find the fairy ring – it was just another five minutes up the trail, and it turned out to be *Agaricus campestris,* the perfectly edible and common meadow mushroom.

Emery picked a couple for lab analysis just to be thorough, and carefully checked over the whole ring.

Nick stood on the trail looking bored now that the adrenaline of his gruesome finding was wearing off. "Do you really have to check every one? They're the same."

"So says the mushroom hunter who stumbles upon a group of similar-looking fungi and foolishly assumes they're all alike," Emery said. Although, to be fair, the likelihood that the mushrooms growing in a ring would be of different species was very rare. Still, she was out here to do a job and she was going to do it well.

It took her about twenty minutes to thoroughly inspect the fairy ring, which was about five feet in diameter and one of the neater specimens she'd come across, with no breaks in the ring—although a few of the stalks were missing their caps—and a number of bright-white, fully mature mushrooms. A welcome sight for foragers, and in this case entirely harmless.

"All right, I guess I have enough samples," Emery said, standing and tucking the meadow mushrooms into the pack at her waist.

"I don't want to say *yay* because that just means we'll have to go back and look at that skeleton again," Nick said. "Any chance I can convince you to just finish the hike? It's a big loop, goes back to the parking lot."

"I promised the detective we'd swing back."

Nick rolled his eyes but started walking.

"Do you think she thinks I had something to do with Brandon's death?" he asked after a few seconds. He seemed incapable of enduring silence.

"I really don't know," Emery said.

"We've been best friends since the third grade," Nick went on. "I was closer to him than my own brothers."

He just kept talking, trying to expel his nervous energy, and Emery could see the anguish in his eyes. Eventually, she mustered a few words of consolation. "If Detective Taylor thought you were a murderer, I doubt she'd let you wander around near the evidence."

Nick nodded. Then he let out a strained laugh and added, "Or be alone with you."

"Yes, let's hope not."

It was easy to find the place where they'd left Julia because when they got back, reinforcements had arrived and were in the process of stringing up yellow caution tape in a wide perimeter around the tree. There was a forensic investigator with a large plastic briefcase preparing to collect evidence.

When Julia spotted Emery, she passed off the caution tape to a woman in a patrol uniform, asking, "Can you take over?"

"Yep, no problem," the officer answered.

Julia climbed up the bank, her cheeks rosy with exertion. "Well?"

"No Amanitas," Emery said. "The fairy ring was edible meadow mushrooms." She pulled the bag out of her pack to show the detective. "And I haven't seen anything on the whole hike that would be lethally toxic. I'll confirm it in the lab, but the worst you'd get from these is a stomachache if you're sensitive."

"And if you're not, you can eat them?"

"Probably not a good idea to eat them raw – that goes for all mushrooms," Emery said. "But yeah, these are as edible as they come."

Julia was nodding along attentively – she was a much better student than the kids Emery had been dealing with lately. Nick was inching his way along the trail, though, trying not to look in the direction of the skeletal remains.

The detective noticed him and said, "Do you want to leave? I think that's all we need from you today."

"That would be *great*," he answered, and practically ran down the trail toward the parking lot.

"Aren't you going to tell him not to leave town?" Emery asked.

"He already got that warning when we talked to him

yesterday," Julia said. "Do you mind sticking around a little bit longer, though? I have some questions while I've got you, but I can't leave yet."

She hooked a thumb in the direction of the investigator and the cop down by the stream, and Emery tried not to smile at her choice of words. *While I've got you...*

You can keep me as long as you like.

"No problem, I'm not expected at the university until after lunch."

"Great," Julia said, pulling out her phone to take notes. "I read the patient chart from the hospital, and talked to the doctor, but it all seemed so chaotic – Hawthorne was pretty much circling the drain by the time he got to the ER. What I don't understand is why he just sat around his apartment and let his liver shut down. What would his symptoms have been?"

"It's possible he thought he was on the mend," Emery said, pleased to be teaching an adult – and to have a few more minutes of admiring Julia's warm brown doe eyes. "If he's not an experienced forager, or he didn't know that he consumed a destroying angel, he likely thought he had a particularly nasty flu, or food poisoning."

She explained the progression of symptoms, something that she fortunately only had theoretical knowledge of.

"It takes a few hours for the poisons to be metabolized and released into the system. You feel fine for six to twelve hours, and then you are very, very not fine," she said. "Food poisoning symptoms – nausea, vomiting, diarrhea – persist for about a day. If you go to the hospital at that stage, you have the best chance at survival. You'll get purgatives and fluids and hopefully flush the toxin out of your system before it has a chance to do any lasting damage to your organs. If you *don't* get treatment, the gastrointestinal symptoms let up after the first day and you start to think you're over it. That lasts another twenty-four to forty-eight hours."

"So we're three days out from consumption now," Julia tallied.

"Yep, and then the really bad turn comes," Emery said. "The GI symptoms resume, and the toxins start to attack the liver, causing major damage that can go on to cause convulsions, coma, death…"

"That's about when Brandon's mom found him," Julia grimaced.

"At that point, it's too late for purgatives and fluids," Emery added. "Liver dialysis may help, but most of the time when it goes that far, the patient needs a liver transplant urgently or they will die."

Julia nodded. "Hawthorne was on the transplant list, he just didn't get a match in time. So you think he started feeling better and got tricked into thinking the worst was over?"

"I'm not a medical doctor so reading his chart wasn't really enough to let me answer that, but it's possible," Emery said.

"So, if he didn't come out here and pick these things himself, where would he have gotten them?" Julia asked. "Somebody had to poison him is all I can figure."

"I was thinking about that," Emery nodded. "Worst-case scenario is a restaurant. Someplace that might still be serving them to unwitting patrons."

"Seriously?" Julia blanched.

"High-end ones often source their ingredients from local sellers," Emery said. "And small-time foragers who sell to restaurants are sometimes just in it for a quick buck. There aren't nearly as many regulations in place as there are for chain restaurants, so you could end up with an inexperienced seller who doesn't know a deadly mushroom from an edible one."

"What a nightmare," Julia said. "And that doesn't even account for the possibility it was intentional. Like those old news stories about people going into pharmacies and tampering with Tylenol bottles."

"There would probably be an awful lot more sick people if this happened on purpose," Emery tried to reassure her.

"Detective?" the officer called from the creek. "Could we get a hand down here?"

"Sure, just a minute," Julia called back. She turned to Emery. "Duty calls. Thank you so much for the information, and for agreeing to come out here today. It's been really helpful." She cast her eyes down toward her shoes as she added, "And sorry again for..."

The phantom sensation of her palms tingled over Emery's breasts.

"Don't worry about it," she said, then dug a business card out of her fanny pack. "Here, in case you have any more questions about the case."

"Thanks." When Julia met her eyes again, she was

smiling, and Emery thought she could see desire dancing in her eyes – maybe she was reliving her near-tumble too?

"I know you already have my office number, but I wrote my cell on the back," Emery added. It was something she pretty regularly did because she didn't always remember to forward her office phone when she left, but something had compelled her to make sure Julia knew that her cell number was there.

Something like the feeling of the detective's hands on her chest, maybe?

Julia flipped the card over, noted the number and shot her a quick, sideways smile. "Got it, I'll call you."

And then she was skidding down the hill toward the investigation scene, and Emery was struggling to keep a stupid smile off her face until after she was out of view. There was chemistry there – she wasn't imagining it… was she?

9
JULIA

Julia was tempted to walk Emery back to the parking lot, if only to spend a bit more time with her. She could always disguise her interest as curiosity about the mushrooms involved in Brandon Hawthorne's death, but the plain truth was that she was immediately attracted to Emery Ellison.

Which was saying something after what Samantha put her through back in Michigan.

She'd fully expected to never fall in love again, or at least require some major therapy first. And yet here she was, definitely more in lust than in love, but feeling *something*.

And a whole lot of it.

In the end, though, a combination of professional duty and morbid curiosity had her sticking around the death scene. She wasn't a forensic investigator, but she damn well wanted to know how the ME's office was planning to get that skeleton out of the tree that had grown all the way around it.

Turned out, the answer was heavy machinery and the forest's second specialist of the day – a forensic anthropologist.

It took most of the day to arrange it all, by the end of which Julia's feet and thighs ached from clambering up and down the hill so many times and her stomach had given up on reminding her that she was hungry. But she got to watch as they chopped the skeletal remains out of the base of the tree, and then dug into the stream bank to free the ball of roots and bones that resulted.

It was a hell of an undertaking and the investigator – who Julia learned was named Tyler – took pictures throughout the process. The whole thing culminated in Tyler painstakingly backing his van down the trail, and all of them working together to load the various pieces of skeletal remains and roots into the vehicle.

It was dark by the time they were all finished, and Julia was exhausted. Her stomach reawakened just as she was sliding behind the steering wheel of her car, relieved to be sitting for the first time all day.

She watched the ME's van make its way back up the trail, and Tyler paused with the window down right beside Julia's car. "You good? Not too tired to drive home?"

"Been a long day but I'm fine, you?"

"Yup," he said. "I'll call you when we know something."

He pulled onto the road, headed back to the ME's office. The patrol officer – Mel – had already left, as had the anthropologist and the lumberjack, so that just left Julia in the parking lot. Suddenly she couldn't wait another minute to get some food in her.

It was that *I would literally kill for a burger* sort of hunger, so she decided to go to the burger joint she'd found near her apartment that was pretty decent. It occurred to her as she drove that both the restaurant and her apartment were not far from the university Emery worked for.

It was called Foster University, which Julia hadn't realized until she saw it on Emery's business card. She'd heard a few people around the station call it Fox U, and as cheeky as it was, she'd assumed that was the actual name.

Julia was tempted to call her now. It was after seven and the chances that Emery would still be in her office were slim. But she *did* have Emery's cell, and Julia hated to eat alone.

She could invite her out for a burger, thank her for her help today. Explore the spark she was sure she'd felt on the trail earlier.

Get herself into a whole new batch of trouble in Pennsylvania to match what she'd left behind in the last state.

Yeah, maybe that wasn't such a good idea.

So she went to the restaurant, ordered a burger to go, scarfed half the French fries before she even got back to her apartment, and ate the rest alone with an episode of *Bones* for company – prompted by the day's crime scene, no doubt.

And went to bed alone – alone was safest.

10
JULIA

The next day, Julia reported to the station and filled everyone in on her gnarly discovery in the woods. All the detectives were just as fascinated as she was, but so far there was no evidence that there'd been foul play.

Julia had called Tom the previous day during a slow moment to tell him what had happened. She resisted the urge to beg to be reassigned to the more interesting case, but he had suggested that she stay in the woods for the day and let him take over the Hawthorne investigation for the day.

It seemed like a fair compromise. There might not even need to be a homicide detective on the tree-skeleton case if the ME determined the death had been natural.

"Dr. Trace has her work cut out for her," Arlen said this morning, shaking her head. "The tree was actually growing *around* the skeleton?"

Julia nodded. "All tangled up – it was wild."

Renee snorted. "Literally wild."

"Well, you've got your work cut out for you today," Tom reminded Julia. "While you were out yesterday, I called Brandon Hawthorne's boss, head coach for the Fox City High boys' baseball team. He said Brandon called off work a couple weeks ago with the flu, he came back a couple days later and acted fine for a day, and then he just stopped showing up."

Julia told him the mycologist had outlined a disease progression that matched that perfectly.

"Note it in the case file," he said.

"She gave me a good lead yesterday, said fancy restaurants sometimes buy foraged mushrooms, so I'm gonna call around and see if any of them have recently made a purchase," Julia added.

"Good," Tom said. "I also tried to reach the girlfriend to no avail, and I called his parents and they're ready to talk. They said they'd come in today – you want to team up on this one?"

"Sure," Julia said. "When?"

Tom checked his watch. "About five minutes."

"Oh shit, let me review my notes." She turned to her computer, tuning out the morning chit-chat going on around her while she worked on pushing yesterday's death scene out of her mind and refreshing herself on her original reason for being in those woods.

She took out Emery Ellison's business card and added it to the case file, and she made a mental note to call and see if anything had come of the samples Emery took yesterday.

What felt like about thirty seconds had gone by when Julia blinked and found Tom standing over her desk, a couple to-go cups of coffee in a cardboard beverage holder his hands. "You ready?"

"It's time?"

He nodded, and Julia stood.

"Ugh, thanks for that, I haven't had any caffeine yet–"

She reached for one of the to-go cups but he held them out of reach and snorted. "These are for the grieving parents. Plan better next time."

Dully noted.

Julia followed him down the hall to a so-called pink room, specially designed to be soothing for victims and family members – as opposed to the stark, discomfort-inducing interrogation rooms used for suspects. It was a lot like the waiting room they'd initially spoken to the Hawthornes in at the hospital – comfortable upholstered furniture, lamps instead of harsh overhead lighting, and yes, light-pink walls believed to produce a calming effect.

Still conspicuous, however, were the hallmarks of a police observation room – tissues, trash can, recording equipment.

The Hawthornes sat together on a sofa, but this time Mrs. Hawthorne wasn't tucked into her husband's side. There was a foot and a half between them, and she sat rigid, her lips pressed into a tight line like she'd shut down her emotions in order to maintain her composure. Julia wondered if she'd done that just for this meeting, or if it was how she was coping at home too.

"Mr. and Mrs. Hawthorne, thanks for coming in," Tom said. "Brought coffee if you'd like it – cream and sugar's there too."

He was taking charge of the interview again, and Julia had to push down her annoyance. She'd been MIA yesterday, working on a more interesting case, but she'd been tricked into thinking Tom was starting to trust her when he let her go out to the woods alone with Nick Wilkins.

Mrs. Hawthorne waved away the coffee with a tight little shake of her head, but Mr. Hawthorne accepted the beverage holder with a *thanks*, setting it on a side table next to him. Julia and Tom took seats across from the sofa, in chairs a lot less cushy and more business-oriented. Julia flipped open her notebook, prepared to play transcriptionist again, and watched as Mr. Hawthorne added sugar to his coffee, his hand shaking slightly. He took a single polite sip before abandoning the cup on the table.

"We're prepared to help however we can, but we're not exactly happy to be here, as I'm sure you can understand. We have a funeral to plan," he said, "so at the risk of being rude, can we please just get this over with?"

"Of course, I understand," Tom said. "If you're ready to talk about it, I'd like to hear more about what happened before Brandon got to the hospital. Mrs. Hawthorne, how was he when you went to check on him?"

"Awful," she said, and the strain of keeping herself together was visible in the tendons pulling at her neck. She didn't cry though, and her voice didn't crack. "I had to use my spare key to get in – he was so weak he couldn't answer the door. I found him in his bedroom, and oh," she wrinkled her nose, remembering, "the stench was *terrible*."

Tom gave her a moment and she breathed deep a couple times, suppressing the sense memory.

"He'd been sick into a trash can beside the bed," she said. "Must have given up on going to the bathroom, or maybe he was too weak to get there."

At that point, her voice did waver, and her husband reached across the expanse between them, setting his hand on hers.

"And before he got sick, thinking back to a few weeks before, he was acting normal?" Tom asked. "Not depressed, sad?"

Julia knew what he was really doing – gently bringing up the possibility of depression, suicide. Yes, the amatoxin had snuck up on him a second time when he thought he was recovering. But there was no record on Brandon's phone of a 911 call, or any attempt at all to reach out for help from a friend, his girlfriend, anyone.

Mr. Hawthorne took over. "He was happy. I know we're the parents, and young people keep secrets from their parents. They don't always say so when they're in trouble... but Brandon was never like that. He always told us when something was wrong."

"There were Gatorade bottles on the nightstand beside the bed," Mrs. Hawthorne said. "Why would he be hydrating if he didn't want to..." she paused, choosing the most palatable euphemism and settling on, "get better?"

"He'd just gotten a promotion to assistant coach," her husband added.

Tom nodded. "I spoke with his boss yesterday. He spoke highly of Brandon. Did he ever mention stress, his new responsibilities weighing on him?"

Again, Mr. Hawthorne shook his head. "He loved that job – being outdoors, coaching kids, it was basically his dream come true." He chuckled. "Well, if you don't count the professional baseball player dream."

"Our son was not suicidal," Mrs. Hawthorne interjected. "He had a good job, a good family. He and Amanda were only dating for a short time but he was already talking like she might be the one. And he had good friends, a supportive family... he was happy."

"I reached out to Amanda, but she hasn't answered her phone," Tom said. "Can you tell me more about her?"

"We didn't have the chance to get to know her too well yet, but she came to see him in the hospital," Mr. Hawthorne said. "We haven't seen her since, but she called yesterday to ask if she can do anything to help with the funeral."

"How long did they date?" Tom prompted.

Mr. Hawthorne looked to his wife. "What's it been, about four months?"

She nodded. "He brought her to meet us for the first time around Christmas. She was a sweet girl. Brandon was so in love with her right from the start."

"Did you ever hear about any fights they had?" Tom asked.

She shook her head, and Mr. Hawthorne took up the mantle. "I think they were still in the honeymoon period – too enamored with each other to fight."

Tom asked a few more questions, and gave Julia the floor to ask anything she wanted. She got a list of restaurants Brandon liked to eat at, but none of them were high-end like Emery told her to look for. Out of respect for the grieving parents, Julia kept her questions to a minimum. The interview ended, Tom said goodbye at the door, and Julia walked them out of the building.

When she got back to her desk, he was sitting at his. He looked up with a grunt.

"Well, that was less than helpful," she said. "Young guy who has everything going for him just lies in bed and dies of severe food poisoning... I'm gonna call around to some restaurants, but do you want to check out the apartment with me in about an hour?"

"Sure," Tom said, "holler when you're ready."

The drive from the police station to Brandon Hawthorne's apartment was only about fifteen minutes, but they took Tom's shiny new SUV, which was a big improvement over the sedan from the motorpool that Julia had been using. It had leather seats – heated for the winter – and it even had hints of that new car smell.

"What do I have to do to get upgraded to one of these?" she asked as they pulled out of the police parking deck.

"Get shot in the line of duty."

Julia damn near choked on her own tongue. "Oh shit."

"It's okay."

"I knew you were injured," she said. "I didn't mean to bring that up."

"It's fine." There was that gruff tone again.

Tom lapsed into silence, and she wondered if she'd fucked things up with him again.

"Now you're thinking the department bribes people who get injured on the job," Tom said.

"No–"

"If they did, I'd have asked for a hell of a lot more than this car," he added. "I don't even get to take it home at night."

He looked sidelong at her, and she realized he was being his version of friendly. Relief washed over her and she relaxed in her seat.

"So, the girlfriend," she said, trying to fill the silence with a new topic. "I tried her just now and I didn't get an answer either."

"Slippery one," Tom agreed. It was the most Julia had felt like she was on equal footing with him since she arrived in Fox County.

They talked more easily the rest of the way to the apartment, which had already been sealed off as a potential crime scene. Evidence technicians had been out to bag up everything in Brandon's refrigerator and pantry that had been opened, plus all of his trash. It was in the forensics lab now, being tested, and if any of it was the source of the amatoxin, the techs would figure it out.

Meanwhile, Julia and Tom did a walk-through of the place. It was as tidy and unhelpful as his parents made it out to be – the apartment of twenty-five-year-old who was mature for his age, responsible, actually ate vegetables and not just an endless supply of frozen meals and take-out pizzas.

There were a few framed photos of Brandon with various people on the TV stand and beside his bed. Julia recognized his parents in one, and Nick Wilkins in another.

The bedroom was as Mrs. Hawthorne described it, too – a sick room with Gatorade bottles and Pepto-Bismol within reach of the bed. There was also an acrid stench, the lingering smells of severe gastrointestinal distress.

"Landlord's gonna have to air this one out," Tom commented.

Julia didn't particularly want to venture into the bedroom – she hadn't thought to bring any camphor with her to disguise the smell. She felt her phone buzz in her pocket and used it as an excuse to wander the living room for a moment, checking the message that had come in.

When she got back, she found Tom in the bedroom. He'd just walked right in and did what he had to, so Julia ignored the smell and did the same.

"Got a call from a restaurant, might have a lead," she

said, then picked up a framed photo by the bedside. "This must be Amanda."

The photo featured Brandon Hawthorne beaming with his arm around a cute blonde in a band tee.

"That's her," Tom nodded. "Found her Facebook profile yesterday – she didn't respond to a message there either."

Julia set the photo frame back down. "Everything the parents said checks out. Doesn't look like the apartment of a guy who was giving up on life."

"Nah, I don't think the kid was suicidal," Tom agreed. "So that rules out one manner of death."

"We're left with accident or homicide," Julia said. "The girlfriend avoiding us isn't looking good. For Brandon's sake, I'm still hoping for accident, though. You up for one more errand before we go back to the station?"

"Restaurant?"

"Yeah, the Chez Lounge has a mushroom guy," she said.

The restaurant wasn't open for dinner service yet when they arrived, but the maître d' heard Julia knocking and came to let them in.

"You spoke to me on the phone," he informed them, leading Julia and Tom through a velvet-upholstered dining room to the kitchen. "This is Chef Elijah, he's the head chef. Elijah, this is the detective I told you called."

The maître d' made himself scarce and Julia sized up

Chef Elijah. He was tall and lanky, with worry lines in his forehead and a decidedly annoyed expression. "I'm not under arrest, am I?"

"No, we just have a few questions," Julia said.

Elijah looked at her, then at Tom. "For me or for the Chez Lounge?"

Ugh, one of those men who ignored her whenever there was another man around because they assumed she had no authority and probably no brain, either. She was too irritated by that attitude to worry about stepping on Tom's toes right now. She stepped subtly in front of him, her gaze burning into Elijah's face until he acknowledged her.

"We're investigating a suspicious death," she said. "They may have eaten at your restaurant."

Elijah put his hands up. "First of all, this isn't *my* restaurant. I just work here."

"But you're the head chef," Julia pressed now that he was on the defensive. "I bet you do all the ordering, like for produce?"

"I do," Elijah says, arms now crossed in front of his chest. "You saying somebody got food poisoning so bad they died?"

She ignored his question. "You have mushrooms on the menu?"

"In some dishes, yeah. Specials, mostly."

"And who do you order them from?"

"We source them locally," he explained. "That's why they're not on the regular menu – they're seasonal for one, and we don't know what we're gonna get until the guy comes."

"Guy?"

"Yeah, mushroom supplier. He shows up when he has something to sell, and we decide if we want it," Elijah said. "Name is... ah... Rick, I think."

A genuine struggle to recall, or was he trying to distance himself from this supplier by pretending not to know him well?

"Is it unusual for a restaurant to get ingredients through that kind of arrangement?" Tom asked.

"At expensive ones, yes," Elijah said. "Certainly not at your local Applebee's." He said the restaurant chain's name like it tasted bad. Then his brow furrowed with those worry lines again. "Are you saying someone died from food they ate at the Chez Lounge? Because if they did, we're going to have to figure out how to deal with the fallout…"

Julia could see his mind working a mile a minute, probably imagining the PR nightmare for the restaurant and how it would look if his name were attached to the news. She held up a hand to stop him before he got too far down that rabbit hole.

"We don't know anything for certain yet, and we'll be sure to notify you if and when we do find something out. For now, it would be really helpful if you could remember Rick the mushroom supplier's last name for me."

"I've got his card somewhere in the office," Elijah said. "Give me a minute."

He disappeared into a small room off the back of the kitchen, and Julia turned to Tom. "What do you think?"

"I think we better pray there's not some get-rich-quick moron out there foraging poison mushrooms and selling them to expensive restaurants," he said. "Chef's right, how the hell would we track down everyone who ate those mushrooms?"

Wait for their livers to fail, Julia thought grimly.

"Here," Elijah said when he returned, holding out a business card.

"Rick Beasley," Julia read. The card was printed on regular printer paper, pointing to a guy who couldn't get his business organized enough to order real business cards. But at least they had contact info now. "Thanks."

Chef Elijah looked relieved to see their backsides as they left the restaurant.

11
EMERY

"What *exactly* are you so smiley about?" Monica asked.

Emery was perched on a lab stool watching Monica run tests on the mushrooms she'd collected from the woods. She was supposed to be doing the heavy lifting – Monica knew what she was doing, but she rarely spent time in the lab unless she had students with her. But after the third time Emery paused with a pipette in hand to tell her yet another detail about her day yesterday, Monica had pushed her out of the way.

"I'm not smiley, I'm just interested in this case."

"Which is why you're letting me do all the work." Monica scoffed. "Come on, I think I know you by now – we've only been colleagues for a decade. You went from worrying about losing your job over that dumb email to drooling on your shoes within twenty-four hours, and we both know there's only one reason for that."

"I need a vacation," Emery said at the same time Monica answered her own question.

"You have a crush on that detective."

Emery bristled. "Do not."

"Yes, you do," she countered. "And summer vacation's right around the corner – comes at the same time every year, so don't use that as an excuse."

"I don't take the summers off," Emery reminded her. She wasn't teaching faculty like Monica, so she worked year-round. Things at the university were always quieter in the summer, and she enjoyed that. More time for serious research. "Anyway, Glen was waiting for me outside my office bright and early this morning."

"Uh-oh. The email?"

"Yeah," Emery said. "I've been avoiding him all week because of it but it wasn't actually that bad of a chewing out. I guess the last community liaison got yelled at by parents all the time. Don't be one of those moms, Monica."

"Not planning on it," she laughed. "And this is exactly why I teach adults."

"The freshmen hardly count," Emery pointed out.

"That's true, but once we get done potty-training them in their first couple years here, most of them become pretty good scientists."

Speaking of which... Emery pointed to the microscope. "Verdict?"

She had a spore print from one of the meadow mushrooms mounted to a slide, and they'd been looking at it on the display monitor mounted above the microscope.

"You seriously don't want to talk about it? I know you're not the gossiping kind, but this is big for you."

Emery arched an eyebrow at her. "You're acting like I've never looked at a woman before."

"Look at them, yes," Monica said. "But actually be more than just friends or colleagues? I can tell this detective is different, the way you talk about her, the way you stare off into the distance and lose your train of thought all the time."

"All the time? It's been one day," Emery said, folding her arms over her chest. "My intentions are not to pick her up, because we're working on this case together and that would be unprofessional."

"But scaring the bejeezus out of a group of ten-year-olds is totally profesh," Monica smiled. Then she turned back to the monitor. "You were right on your ID. Plain old meadow mushrooms." She gave Emery a wink. "There, your part in the case is finished, so you can ask her out."

Emery took off the latex gloves she was wearing and snapped them in Monica's direction.

"I'm going to my office to write this up," she said. "Send me screenshots of those spore prints."

"You're the boss... when Glen's not around."

Emery went down the hall to her office and shut the door behind her. She turned on the task light at her desk instead of the overhead, partly because it was a nice, sunny day out, and partly because it helped her avoid Glen, which was always a good thing.

She was halfway through writing up her findings on

both the hike and the harmless meadow mushrooms she found when her desk phone rang. Figuring it was Monica wanting to go to lunch, Emery picked up and tucked the receiver against her shoulder. "This is Dr. Ellison."

"No, this is Patrick," was the reply she was waiting for – Monica's go-to *Spongebob* reference whenever she called Emery.

Instead, there was a pause, a throat clearing, and a surprising voice tickling her ear. "Hi, this is Detective Julia Taylor... from yesterday."

A smile came automatically to Emery's lips and suddenly all of her attention was on her caller. "Yes, I remember... you made a strong, uh, *impression* on me."

"Oh god," Julia laughed. "You're never going to let me live that down, are you?"

"I really don't see that happening."

Julia cleared her throat again. "Well, the reason I'm calling is I wanted to thank you for the restaurant lead... and check on your findings... although it was just yesterday that you collected those specimens... and you probably have a lot more to do than just consult for me..."

She was rambling and it was totally something Emery would have done. It instantly charmed her, and she decided to let Julia keep rambling simply because she wanted to know how long it would go on for. She wanted to keep hearing that soft, sweet voice in her ear.

"You know what?" Julia cut herself off abruptly, her tone shifting. "The truth is that my boss just left me on my own for lunch and I can't stop thinking about you – you're really cute and interesting, and I'd love to learn more about what a mycologist does. Do you want to grab something to eat?"

Emery opened her mouth to say yes, but Julia proved not quite finished.

"Oh man, you probably have a wife," she second-guessed herself. "I bet you don't wear a ring because you work in a lab and it's dangerous, and I shouldn't even be thinking about women like that right now, and–"

"I don't have a wife," Emery cut her off, finally saving her from herself. "And I'd love to get lunch with you. Where?"

She heard Julia sigh as if her tension valve had been released. Emery could picture the big smile on her face. "I have to stay close to the station in case there are any developments. There's a diner not far from here that's good."

"Sounds great, what's it called?"

Julia gave her directions, and Emery hung up the phone feeling pleased with herself – even if it did mean Monica was right about everything she'd said in the lab. Julia liked her, and it was time to put herself out there a little more.

Well, Emery just wouldn't tell Monica about her win – not right away, anyhow.

12
JULIA

It was pretty much noon on the dot, and despite having a breakfast-oriented menu, the diner was busy. Julia walked there and grabbed the last available booth, marveling at the fact that she was about to have lunch with a gorgeous scientist.

Just a couple weeks ago, she would have sat at her desk with a take-out sandwich. She definitely wouldn't have had the guts to call Emery out of the blue. She was opening a can of worms with someone she didn't know very well, but once she got on the phone with her, she had to take her shot.

Maybe things would be different here. Better.

When she saw Emery step into the diner, Julia waved her over. She was out of her hiking gear today, looking professorial in a pair of slim-fitting black slacks and a plaid button-down shirt, sleeves rolled to the elbows and a messenger bag draped across her chest. Her dimples were just as adorable here as they'd been in the early morning sun, and Julia felt a tingle in her core just sitting across from her.

"Thanks for meeting me," she said. "I hate eating alone."

"I don't mind it – I do it a lot," Emery said. "Although having company is better, as long as it's the right kind."

"I'll try my hardest to be that," Julia said. Something about Emery made Julia want to impress her – easier yesterday when she was in her element, even when she was tripping and making a fool of herself.

"You don't have to try at all," Emery said. Then she lifted her menu.

Julia ordered an omelet, something that wouldn't sit heavily in her belly all afternoon. Emery had a salad, and they worked together to drain two carafes of coffee over the course of the meal.

"I brought my report on my findings," Emery said as soon as the server took their orders. She pulled a manilla folder out of her bag and handed it to Julia. "It's not the final-final version, I had to rush to finish after you called, but I figured you'd want to take a look."

Julia flipped the folder open, frowning at all the technical language, the microscope images depicting scientists-only-knew what. "Mind giving me the Cliff's Notes version for the scientifically disinclined?"

Emery explained it all to her in great detail, and it was clear she was enjoying the process. Julia enjoyed it too, the way Emery leaned over the table, the fresh lemongrass scent of her clothes wafting over, her eyes meeting Julia's in furtive glances. Their fingers brushed each other a couple of times – accidentally at first, but Julia started finding reasons to point at the report.

"And this? What does this chart mean?"

The conversation drew out, probably longer than it needed to for something that really boiled down to *nothing pertinent to the case was found in the woods*. But it got them to when their food arrived without any awkward silences, and then Emery tucked the report back into the manilla envelope and handed it to Julia.

She took it, then popped a piece of bacon in her mouth. With her cheek full, she said, "Oh, I wanted to tell you about my restaurant lead – thanks for that tip."

"What did you find?"

"There was only one restaurant I could track down in the area that's recently purchased mushrooms from a guy named..." She plucked the name from the long list of new ones floating around in her head. "Rick Beasley. Left him a voicemail just before I came here, hopefully he calls me back today so we can chat."

Emery's eyes lit up. "I know Rick, pretty well, actually."

"Really?"

"Yep. The mycology community is pretty tight-knit."

"That so?" Julia was smiling cheekily at her, enjoying the view from across the booth.

"The mycology community in the entire United States isn't that big, truth be told, and Fox County is an even smaller world," Emery explained. "I met Rick years ago at a talk given by my predecessor at the university, and he sends the department questions every once in a while."

"So you think he knows what he's doing?"

"Definitely," Emery went on. "He may be kind of an old hippie who does things on his own schedule, but he's been foraging for decades now. There's no way he'd accidentally sell someone a destroying angel."

"Well, damn." Julia put down her next slice of bacon. "I guess that brings me back to square one."

"Sorry."

"It's okay, I'm used to working hard," Julia said.

"So, you mentioned while we were hiking that you're new to the area," Emery said as she drizzled vinaigrette over her salad. "What made you move to Fox City?"

"The foxy ladies, of course," Julia said, emboldened by the way Emery was looking at her.

"There *are* a lot of them in the police department," Emery said. "I've only consulted on one other case – I just became the community liaison at the beginning of the school year – but I've met a few."

Jealousy surged hot, sour and quick in Julia's belly, and she pushed it aside as ridiculous.

"Oh yeah? Seeing any of them?"

Real smooth… but there was no point letting this crush get any bigger if the sexy mycologist sitting across from her was taken.

Emery smiled, coy as hell. "No."

She was going to make Julia drag it out of her.

"Someone at the university, then?"

"No."

Her eyes were dancing with mischief, and Julia was pretty sure she was going to die if the answer ended up being yes, Emery's taken, when she finally asked the right question.

"Wife?" she cut to the chase. "Girlfriend?"

"No and no," Emery said. "You?"

Julia's heart did a quick double-time in her chest before returning to normal. Her pulse, on the other hand, stayed elevated. She shook her head and took a big bite of her omelet.

"Did you leave a broken heart somewhere back in Michigan?" Emery asked.

Julia had to stifle a snort. "Yes, but not how you think."

"Oh?"

How much did she want to tell her? How much did she dare share before it would – rightly – scare Emery off?

"The broken heart was my own," she said. Shattered to pieces with so little left of it that it wasn't worth schlepping across state lines. "The relationship was... not a good one."

"Toxic?"

"To put it mildly," Julia answered. "But that's not great lunch conversation... why don't you tell me about yourself instead? I've gotta confess, I'm dying to know what a fascinating woman like you does in her free time – you must have some interesting hobbies."

"Fascinating?" Emery's eyebrow arched in disagreement.

"You study mushrooms, you're not the least bit squeamish when you stumble across a skeleton in the woods, and you confidently rock a fanny pack better than anyone I've ever seen – nineteen-eighties inclusive."

Emery laughed. "What do you know of the eighties? Were you even born then?"

"Ninety-five," Julia admitted. She'd never commit the cardinal sin of asking a woman her age, but if she had to guess, she'd say Emery had about ten years on her.

It didn't bother Julia in the least, but that sentiment didn't always go the other way.

"Eighty-three here," Emery volunteered. "I was seven when the eighties ended so I guess I wasn't a fashion expert at the time. I just appreciate the utility of a fanny pack when I'm out collecting specimens, without the bulk of a backpack. Oh, and they're called belt bags now."

"I always thought they were extremely nerdy," Julia teased, "until I saw you in one."

"Then you *knew* they were extremely nerdy," Emery answered with a wide grin. "And I no longer want to share my hobby with you because I'm afraid that, coupled with the belt bag, it'll make me simply too geeky. One of two things will happen."

She let it hang, and Julia found herself leaning forward in her seat. "And those are?"

"One, you will find me entirely irresistible and climb across this table to beg me to ravish you, thus getting us kicked out of this fine establishment," Emery said, her delivery deadpan and yet incredibly sexy. "Or two, you will make a beeline for the nearest exit, we'll never speak again, and you'll always think of me as 'that weird scientist.'"

"I'm intrigued by option one," Julia said, her pulse still racing through her veins. She never would have guessed she'd be ready for this kind of banter so soon after Samantha. Should be running from it, really. But part of her *did* want to crawl across the table and into Emery's lap. "What's your hobby?"

Emery laughed. "I can see it in your eyes – you're chanting *don't let it be taxidermy* in your head, aren't you?"

"Come *on*," Julia begged. "Just tell me!"

"Spider web preservation," Emery said, and Julia sat back.

"Wow, I don't even know what that is but I never in a million years would have guessed it." She sipped her coffee, omelet all but forgotten. "Tell me more."

Apparently, spider web preservation was part hunting, part scrapbooking. It involved hiking through the woods until Emery found a good specimen – preferably one that was a little dusty, indicating that the spider had moved on. Then she'd spray it with adhesive and press it against a black piece of heavy-duty cardstock to collect it.

"What do you do with them?" Julia asked. "I *told* you that you were fascinating, by the way, and this just proves it. I've never even heard of this before."

"My dad taught me how to do it when I was a kid," Emery explained. "He was an entomologist, retired now, and while bugs aren't really my thing, he got me interested in nature. Now I mostly just do it as an excuse to go exploring, but if I get a really good one, I frame it up and give it as a gift."

"Well, if you're ever my Secret Santa, I'd love one," Julia said. "My apartment walls are completely bare right now – crying out for some weird art. Oh – not that it's weird–"

Emery laughed. "It's totally weird. And beautiful too, they make great conversation pieces. When I go home tonight, I'll pick one out from my collection that I think you'll like."

Julia's cheeks colored, and the fact that they now had another reason to meet did not escape her.

"What about you?" Emery asked. "What's your most remarkable hobby?"

"I feel like a potato next to you," Julia admitted. "Anything I say will be boring in comparison."

Emery shook her head. "You think I'm fascinating? Well, you're an enigma to me, and I find that just as compelling." Her foot nudged Julia's under the table – on purpose? "I'm a scientist, after all – it's in my nature to be intrigued by new and interesting things, and you *are* interesting."

Julia's heart was in her throat again. This time, it was at the idea of Emery studying her like she studied her mushrooms – looking at her under a microscope, figuring out all her secrets. Things no one in Fox County knew, things she didn't want them to find out.

Maybe this was a bad idea after all.

"I wanted to be an Olympic figure skater when I was

a kid," she said. "I was good, too. But it didn't go anywhere. My parents couldn't afford coaching, and even if they could, they didn't have time to drive me to practice for hours every day, which is what you have to do if you want to compete on that level. Now I just skate for fun when I can."

Emery's eyes glimmered. "See? That's very interesting and I have follow-up questions."

Julia's phone started to vibrate against her hip. "Oh, hold that thought."

As she extracted the phone from her pocket, it suddenly occurred to her that they'd been sitting here talking for an awfully long time – long enough for the server to come back for several coffee refills, long enough for her untouched omelet to go cold.

Long enough for her to be late getting back to the station.

When she saw *Tom Logan* on her screen, she cursed.

"What's wrong?" Emery asked.

Julia answered and before she could even finish her *hello*, he was asking, "Taking a long lunch?"

"I'm so sorry–"

"Amanda Drake showed up. I've got her waiting right now but I'll do the job myself if you're not here in five minutes."

He hung up, and Julia stood, nearly knocking her coffee over in the process. "Shit, shit, shit, I gotta go. I lost track of time."

Emery stood with her. "Go – I'll take care of the bill."

"Are you sure?"

"I got this," she said, though a smile flickered across her lips. "Although that does qualify this as a date."

If she could have stuck around long enough to acknowledge it, Julia would have gotten flustered, maybe blushed, probably started worrying again and wondering whether any of this was a smart idea.

Another part of her would have wanted to kiss Emery, and she was pretty sure Emery wanted that too.

13
JULIA

When Julia arrived back at the station, out of breath and her dark hair frizzy around her temples from running, Tom wasn't at his desk. Arlen looked unimpressed but told Julia he was already in the room with Amanda and that Tom said she could go in.

He'd taken Amanda to one of the interrogation rooms rather than the pink room. That meant he was looking at her as a potential suspect, and Julia had to agree. The phrase they used on crime shows all the time, "It's always the spouse," was generally true, especially ones as hard to track down as Amanda Drake.

Julia paused outside the door for a moment, catching her breath, smoothing her hair and shifting her brain from the lovey mush it had been sitting across from Emery and back into professional mode.

Then she stepped inside.

Tom was sitting across from Amanda, who was young and blonde and cradled a to-go cup of coffee in her hands. Her eyes were red-rimmed, and if she wasn't genuinely distraught at the death of her boyfriend, she was doing a really good job of pretending.

"This is Detective Taylor," Tom said, successfully disguising his own annoyance at how late Julia was. "She's been *assisting* on this case."

Damn it. Demoted to assistant again.

"Hi," Amanda said blankly, holding out a hand.

Julia shook it, then took a seat in a chair pushed up against the wall, away from the stainless-steel table. *Silent observer* seemed to be the best role for her to play right now, so she flipped open her notebook and clicked her pen, ready to take notes.

Tom turned back to Amanda. "You were telling me about the last time you saw Brandon."

"It was about two weeks before he died... well, if you don't count when he was in the hospital," she said. "I visited him there, but they'd induced a coma so I couldn't really talk to him."

"Was that typical?" Tom asked gently. "To go a week or two between seeing him?"

"No," Amanda said. "Normally I see... saw... him every day, or as often as we could with our schedules. He thought he had a stomach bug – he didn't want me to catch it."

"So he told you not to visit?"

"Yeah, he said he'd call me when he was feeling better," she said. "We texted and Facetimed while he was sick, and at one point he thought he was better, so we made plans to go to dinner at our favorite restaurant the next night."

"Where?" Tom pounced on the detail, and Julia figured he was hoping for another lead on the source of the toxic mushrooms.

But Amanda shook her head. "This little diner down the street from his apartment, but we never made it there. He got sick again and cancelled. I shoulda gone over there, checked on him. But he asked me to give him space and I was trying to honor his wishes. His mom found him," she said. "It could have been me, and it coulda been *days* earlier. Maybe that would have made the difference."

Julia couldn't dispute that – Emery told that early intervention was a person's best chance against amatoxin. But there was no reason to let this girl sit here and beat herself up over something she couldn't change. Julia grabbed a box of tissues – ubiquitous all over the police station – and passed them to her.

"Thank you," Amanda murmured into one.

"And where have you been the past few days?" Julia asked. Tom may have already asked the question before she got here, but Amanda could answer it again.

"Mourning," Amanda shot her a sharp look. "My boyfriend died."

"You didn't answer your phone despite multiple calls from the police," Julia pressed. "And you didn't answer your door when I sent an officer to check your apartment."

"I've been going out walking a lot," she said, "trying

to process all this. Excuse me if I've been too upset to look at my damn phone."

"What about work, been too busy mourning to go to work?" Julia pressed.

Amanda nibbled her lip, then said, "No, I went to work."

"And where is that?"

Amanda told them the name of a meal delivery service, and Julia wrote it down.

"What do you do there?"

"I'm a prep cook," she said. "Trying to work my way up the ladder. It's one of the reasons Brandon didn't want me to visit him while he was sick – I can't afford to get on my boss's bad side if I want to move up."

"I'm going to reach out to your boss – will he have good things to say about you? Say you've been to all your shifts lately?"

Amanda glowered at her. "Yes, he will. I loved Brandon. I had nothing to do with his death."

The interview wasn't a long one. Julia and Tom asked all the questions they had, and Amanda made it clear from the outset that she was doing them a favor showing up to talk in the first place. They walked her to the elevators, and as soon as the doors slid closed on Amanda Drake, Tom turned to Julia. "So, she seems emotional, but I didn't hear any glaring red flags."

"Apart from being damn hard to contact," she added. "And getting a bit snippy with me at the end there."

"Yeah, but everyone grieves differently," Tom said.

"Can't really establish an alibi for her, or anyone else

for that matter, considering Brandon could have been poisoned at any time roughly two weeks ago," Julia said, "but I'll go call Amanda's workplace right now, see if she's missed any shifts in the last few weeks."

"Have you reached out to her parents?" Tom asked.

"Left them a voicemail," Julia said. "Waiting to hear back."

"Ah, so the 'hard to reach' thing is genetic," Tom grunted. "Well, we've got a dead man, a known poison, no motivation and no strong suspects."

"I won't rest until I crack this," Julia said, and Tom shot her a *simmer down* look.

"Take it easy, hot shot. You don't want to burn out in your first week. Speaking of, where the hell were you?"

"I was down the street at the diner eating with the mycologist, Dr. Ellison," Julia said. "I lost track of time."

"Lost track of time, huh?"

She could tell from the look in his eyes he was inferring things she'd rather he didn't. Of course she couldn't make casual reference to a lunch date around here without raising suspicions – she shouldn't have even mentioned Emery.

"Yes, I'm sorry," she said.

"Business or pleasure?"

Julia's cheeks colored. She could try to claim the lunch had been all business, but that would be a lie. "I don't believe it's against department policy – she's a consultant, not a county employee–"

"Not why I was asking," Tom said, holding up a hand to stop her. "But now that you mention it, probably best if you hold off until her involvement in the case has ended. If this ends up going to trial, we don't want to give the defense any ammo regarding conflict of interest."

"You're right," Julia sighed.

"Hey, buck up," Tom added. "It's not your fault, there's something in the water around here, I swear."

14
JULIA

On Friday afternoon, Julia was looking at a very long, boring weekend ahead of her. It stretched uncomfortably in front of her as she slowly – oh, so slowly – organized the files on her desk and tidied up for the weekend.

Her apartment was still very empty. She'd finished unpacking all her boxes last weekend – which just went to prove how bored she'd been. All there was to do when she wasn't working was think... and she didn't particularly enjoy being in her own head at the moment.

Not with the aftermath of her ex, Samantha, rattling around in there. They'd only dated for about six months before Julia realized Sam was frighteningly possessive and she didn't want any part of it. She'd broken it off almost a year ago and Sam should have been so far in her rear-view mirror by now she was just a speck.

Instead, Julia was still jumping at shadows, expecting

Sam to pop up around every corner. Even with three hundred miles between them, Sam still haunted her.

Julia had locked her stack of open case files in a drawer and straightened her pencil cup twice, and was just reaching the conclusion that there was nothing to do but clock out and go home, when Tate came over to her desk.

"Taphouse?"

"Huh?" Julia asked.

"I'm going with Ariel and Lena," said Tate. She'd been the second to go out on a case with Arlen, after Renee finished up her case concerning the slip-and-fall mid-week, and she seemed like the most outgoing of the new detectives.

"Is it a bar?" Julia asked.

"Yeah," Tate said with a smile. She had dark brown eyes and medium-length straight hair to match, which she usually kept in a tight bun at the base of her neck. She had an ex-military vibe about her, but managed to be friendly at the same time as she was rigid and precise. "Lots of the county workers go there for drinks at the end of the week. Detective Rose told us we should come too. Sorry, I assumed Logan filled you in."

"He's not the most talkative guy," Julia said. Not to mention the fact that it felt like every time she turned around this week, she'd found a way to get on his bad side. She wasn't going to hold her breath for an invitation to hang out. "Will Renee be there?"

Tate rolled her eyes. "I don't know why you two got

off on the wrong foot, but she's not so bad. Just come – be social."

"Okay."

Tate didn't exactly have to drag her there – any excuse not to sit alone in her apartment was a good one, and she'd have to start making friends in the department eventually. Tonight was as good a night as any for it.

"Leave your car in the parking garage – Arlen says it's walkable from here," Tate said as Ariel and Lena came over to join them.

"We're going to buddy up with a rideshare when it's time to go home, right?" Lena asked. "I know that creep's in prison, but it still freaks me out that I coulda been in his car and not even known it."

"Creep?" Julia asked.

"Oh boy, you don't know?" Lena asked.

"She was in another state at the time," Ariel reminded her.

"It was national news," Lena said. "The rideshare creep? Guy who was abducting the women who got in his car? He did it for *years* before they caught him last spring. One of the forensic investigators got kidnapped right out of the ME's office!"

"That's nuts," Julia said, a chill running up her spine.

"Histologist," Ariel added.

"Huh?"

"It was the histologist, Elise, not an investigator."

"Oh. Well, I was kinda busy last spring," Julia mumbled. "Guess I missed the news."

Not a good excuse for missing a major crime spree,

especially as a homicide detective, but everyone was eager to get to the Taphouse and unwind, and they moved on to other topics.

By the time they arrived, they'd covered their previous jobs and assignments, their first impressions of the station, and interesting tidbits from their cases this week. The star was, of course, the skeleton tangled in tree roots, which Renee had taken over. She was coming from the ME's office after watching the autopsy for that case and planning to meet everyone at the bar, so they were eager to hear what more she could report.

"Tom and I are at a dead-end with the mushroom poisoning case," Julia said. "Skeleton-eaten-by-tree is interesting, but I have to agree with him, between the two cases, the mushroom toxicity is far more likely to be foul play."

"Yeah, but *skeleton eaten by tree,*" Ariel said.

Julia laughed. "I know!"

They went into the bar, which was crowded even though it was just after five. A jukebox played at just the right volume to still be able to hold a conversation, and Julia could smell something mouth-watering and deep-fried wafting out of the kitchen at the back of the bar.

A hand shot up at a cluster of bar-height tables in the corner, and she spotted Arlen with her arm around the shoulder of her girlfriend, the investigator Julia had met at the hospital on her first day with Tom.

"There they are," Tate said, leading the way.

They threaded through the room single-file, Julia bringing up the rear, and when she reached the table, she saw a few more women she didn't know, both in and out of uniform, plus Renee.

Who looked about as pleased to see her as Julia was.

She had her foot up on the rung of one of the bar stools, and she grudgingly shoved the chair out for Julia. "Get enough one-on-one time with Logan this week?"

"Too much," Julia said, sitting. "I think he hates me."

Renee smirked, but Arlen said, "He doesn't hate you – he's just gruff on the outside."

"And sometimes on the inside too," a masculine-of-center woman with dark ebony skin said, then leaned across the table with her hand out. "I'm Zara. I work narcotics."

"Julia, homicide."

They shook hands, and Zara went around the table shaking hands with all the new arrivals, getting their names. Then she sat back, cozying up to a cute, curvy woman in an A-line dress. Julia guessed *not* police, because none of the detectives she knew chose anything but pants. You never knew when you'd have to run, or hike through the woods, or anything else where a dress would present problems.

"This is my fiancée, Kelsey," Zara said. "And that's Dylan and her partner, Elise. All three of them work at the medical examiner's office."

Elise – one of the rideshare creep's kidnapping victims, very lucky to have escaped becoming part of his body count. She looked happy, perfectly comfortable with one hand resting on her partner's knee, the other one holding a beer. How could she be so well-adjusted after going through something like that?

Julia had changed her name, moved to a new state and installed extra locks on her apartment door just to avoid her ex-girlfriend.

"Get you a drink?"

The bartender had come over, and left a couple minutes later with nearly a dozen drink orders in her head. She hadn't written a thing down, and yet she returned with everything perfectly arranged on a tray.

Once they all had something to sip on, the unwinding portion of the evening got underway. They unloaded the stress of the week, talked about their plans for the weekend, got to know each other.

Julia was mostly quiet, nursing a beer that she'd selected hastily based on the taps she could read from across the bar. It wasn't bad, but her heart wasn't in it – much like the conversation going on around her. She wanted to fit in here, to make this her new home, but it all felt so temporary.

Like it could be snatched away from her at any moment.

The only time it didn't feel like that, in fact, was when she was with Emery. Whenever that woman was around, Julia was a hundred percent invested in the moment.

"What about you, Taylor?" Renee surprised her by directing the conversation her way. "What made you move here?"

A crazy bitch who woke up one morning and decided

to destroy my whole world, Julia would have said if she didn't have such a fine-tuned filter on her mouth. That thing was rock-solid, though, and instead she said, "I just needed a change. New town, new people. And I heard good things about FCPD."

"Bad break-up?" Elise guessed.

Julia snorted. "How did you know?"

"That's gotta be in the top three reasons to flee a state," she said.

"Number one, felon on the run," her partner chimed in. "Number two, moving to be with someone."

"Which one is it for you, Tate?" Lena asked.

"Felon, obviously."

"What, does Fox County not even bother running background checks?" Ariel asked.

"I need another," Julia interrupted, draining the last of her beer. "Anyone else?"

"I'll take one, Mike's Hard," Renee said.

Julia slid off her bar stool, taking her time to flag down the bartender and get a couple fresh bottles. Her heartrate had spiked the minute they started talking about her past. She couldn't bring her old name to Fox County or Sam would have followed her immediately and she may as well have never moved. But showing up in a new city with no past, and working with a bunch of detectives?

It was no wonder Renee looked at her with suspicion from the start, and was constantly asking pointed questions like that.

It'd be an easy enough solution to just explain to her

new team why Julia Taylor had no history, that she'd changed her name to escape a stalker ex. She'd probably even get some sympathy out of it.

But Julia couldn't ignore the nagging little voice in her head that said the minute she told *anyone* here her real name, the connection would be forged. And Samantha, persistent as she was, would figure it out sooner or later.

And show up on her doorstep as soon as she did.

Julia damn near just walked right out the door. She was dying for some fresh air and she suddenly didn't feel like socializing at all – even if it meant going back to her empty, lonely apartment. She might have, if not for the fact that Renee was waiting for her stupid Mike's Hard Lemonade.

So she went back to the group, gave Renee her drink, and did her best to fade back into the background while she listened to Lena and Ariel talk about a band coming to Fox City in a couple weeks that they wanted to see. Julia's heartrate slowly inched back down to within the normal range, and the alcohol hitting her bloodstream did its part to relax her.

Soon, she was even having fun.

"Can we talk about Tom, please?" she asked Arlen once she was sufficiently loosened up. "I see evidence of him being friendly with other people. How do I get him to like me?"

Without the benefit of alcohol, she never would have exposed a nerve like that. But half the people around this table had friendly relationships with the guy she'd just spent most of her work week with. She really wanted to know.

"You just have to give him time," Arlen said. "He's a grumpy bastard, but he warms up to people once he knows he can trust them to do their jobs."

I haven't done that already? Julia pouted. Sure, there was the thing with Amanda Drake, walking into the interview ten minutes late, but she'd been on her lunch break.

After a while, Zara, Kelsey, Dylan, Elise, Arlen and Maya decided that they'd had enough, and Dylan took Maya's keys. "I'm DDing. Do you all want a ride too?"

"No, I'm going to stay a bit longer," Lena said. "One more round?"

Ariel, Renee and Tate said yes, so Julia did too. These were her new coworkers – whether her boss liked her or not, she needed to get to know them, be tight with them. Rely on them.

"Well, promise not to take a rideshare, okay?" Elise said. "You can call Dylan when you're ready to go if you need a sober driver, right, babe?"

"Of course."

"It's okay, I actually don't drink," Ariel said, pointing to the lemonade sitting in front of her. "I'll drive."

They saw the largest part of the group off, Lena went to the bar to get everyone one more drink, and they settled in. Things were awkwardly quiet for a moment as they got used to the new group dynamic.

Then Ariel said, "Okay, I've been meaning to ask since training but I didn't want to be that awkward coworker... who wants to be Facebook friends with me?"

"Sure," Lena said immediately. "My profile's public, you should be able to find me."

Phones came out around the table, and sweat popped out on Julia's brow. She'd scoured the internet deleting all the profiles she could think of under her old name – anything Samantha could possibly use to track her down. But you couldn't just create a new profile overnight, at least not one that wasn't suspiciously empty of posts and friends, so she hadn't bothered.

And if you weren't on the internet... were you even real?

"What about you, Julia?" Ariel asked. "I'm not seeing you."

"Umm, I think I set my profile to private," she said, buying time.

"Did you?" Renee asked, eyebrow arched. Lord, Julia wanted to knock her off her barstool.

"Yes," she said through gritted teeth. "Gimme a minute."

"Okay – there's a few Ariel Sterners. I'm the one with the orchid profile pic," she said, then stared at Julia expectantly.

Oh, right, phone. She dug it out of her pocket and opened Facebook, met with a login screen. "Just a sec..."

How exactly was she going to get out of this? Even if she could surreptitiously create an account right here at the table, they'd all know it was new the instant they saw that she had no friends, no photos, no profile posts.

You should have just said you don't do Facebook!

Yes, that would have been a good idea two minutes ago... She was having an argument with her own internal monolog, all the while also cursing the alcohol making her brain feel like sludge and frantically trying to think of a way out of this.

"Wait, is this you?"

Tate held up her phone. Julia frowned. Did Facebook not follow through with deleting her profile like she asked? She dragged her eyes over to Tate's screen. She must have googled Julia, because it wasn't a Facebook account but her old LinkedIn profile that was staring her in the face.

Fucking LinkedIn!

She forgot that one. When was the last time she'd even used it? Not since she applied for her first patrol job in Michigan, ages ago. They always told her when she was in college that she needed a LinkedIn profile, and yet this was all it ever got her.

Her real name screamed at her from across the bar table.

How had she even found that profile? Had to be the stupid connections, a cop they both knew, something like that. Damn it! What if Sam had found this profile too and traced her way down to Ohio?

"Frances Martin?" Ariel read.

Julia shrugged. Her brain had fully shut down now, deciding not to help her out with this at all, and she had to resort to crude gestures instead. "Not me."

"It looks like you," Tate insisted.

"Lemme see that," Renee said, looking over Tate's shoulder.

"I guess I just have that kinda face," Julia said. The profile pic was over a decade old and at the time she thought she was being mysterious and clever by using a black and white headshot. So at least she had that going for her – but it was a flimsy excuse and she knew it. She slid off her stool. "I just remembered I told my sister I was gonna call her tonight. She probably thinks I'm dead – gotta go."

Sister?! Way to dig yourself in deeper, dummy!

As sure as that LinkedIn profile was hers, Julia did not have a sister. The fewer relatives she'd had to account for, the easier it had been to make Frances Martin disappear... but now she was inventing them for her new identity!

This couldn't end well.

15
EMERY

Very little about Emery's job was ever so urgent that she received calls in the middle of the night.

Even when she went on a rare vacation, her work just piled up on her desk, left for her to deal with when she came back.

But tonight, she was awoken from a dead sleep by the shrill sound of her work ringer cutting through the darkness. She'd set it to something grating just to make sure that she never accidentally missed a work call, but this was the first time she ever regretted it. Her brain was fuzzy and panicked when she fumbled her phone off the nightstand and jabbed at the *Answer* button.

"H'lo?"

"It's Glen," her boss said.

Oh shit.

"Were you asleep?"

Emery held the phone out, squinting at the painfully

bright screen. Two in the morning. She held it back to her ear. "Uh, yes, but that's okay."

She grimaced at the pandering tone coming out of her mouth. Even at this hour, it was ready to come out when anyone in authority spoke to her – even Glen.

"Sorry," he said, not sounding it. "There's another suspected amatoxin poisoning case."

That got her awake. Emery sat up. "Deceased?"

"I wouldn't be calling you at two in the morning if he was dead," Glen said, and if she *was* still half-asleep, she would have pointed out the nerve it took to call her and then be the one to serve up sass. "He's at Fox County Hospital. They're treating him as if it's amatoxin, but they need an analysis of the mushrooms he ate ASAP."

"I believe that's 'stat' in medical terms," Emery said. Okay, so maybe her filter wasn't fully operational just yet.

"Right," he said, annoyed. "Can you go down there and get the sample, then run the tests? I told them it'd be faster that way since we know exactly what to look for, and you're closer to the hospital than me."

Technically true, but Emery was pretty sure it also had something to do with Glen's desire to go back to sleep after this call ended. He would call it seniority, or delegation. Fancy words for passing the buck – his favorite managerial task.

"Yes," she said. "I'm on my way."

Or at least she was out of bed now, looking around for something other than PJs to wear.

"Emergency room," Glen said. "Patient's name is Kyle Brogan."

Emery pulled on jeans, mumbling, "I'll be right there."

"Okay, keep me posted," Glen said, then thought better of it. "Actually, shoot me an email if it's before eight."

"You got it, boss," she said, and she even managed to roll her eyes without that attitude leaking into her tone.

It wasn't until Emery was pulling into the parking lot outside the emergency room that it occurred to her she might run into a certain detective in there. They would have called Julia about this, right? There was no way this poisoning was unrelated to the last one if it really was amatoxin – there were only a handful of Amanita deaths every year across the whole country. Two in one county within a week? Emery didn't believe in that kind of coincidence.

She parked and spared a fast glance in the rearview mirror. How bad was it? Well, she was still wearing her hair wrap, for one thing. She yanked it off and ran her fingers through her hair to tame it as best she could as she went inside.

"I'm Dr. Ellison, the mycologist here for Kyle Brogan," she told the first person in scrubs that she saw.

"Bed six," the man said, pointing her to a row of hospital beds along one side of the emergency room. A couple were empty. One contained a kid receiving a breathing treatment. And the last one in the row had its curtain pulled shut.

Emery's heart was pounding, and not just from how fast she'd raced here. She belonged in a lab – she wasn't the community liaison type, and she didn't know how to handle all this.

If she didn't figure it out fast, though, Kyle Brogan could die just like Brandon Hawthorne had.

She walked up to bed six, thought it would be polite to knock, but on what? The curtain? And so she just pulled it aside.

Inside, a familiar face was waiting for her. Julia was standing beside the hospital bed, and the way her eyes lit up the moment their gazes met made Emery's heartbeat slow by a few increments.

"Hi," she said.

"Hi." Emery knew there was a goofy smile on her face, but she couldn't wipe it away. She'd been thinking about this gorgeous woman ever since the diner, wondering if she'd gotten her in trouble with her boss, wondering if it would be too clingy if she were to text her.

The sound of gagging interrupted their reunion, drawing Emery's attention to the reason she was here in the early hours of the morning. Kyle Brogan was vomiting violently, and another person in scrubs was on the other side of the bed tending to him. Judging from the fact that he was holding the emesis basin, Emery guessed he was a nurse, not an ER doc.

"Why aren't the anti-emetics working?" Kyle groaned when he finished and caught his breath.

"Because you have to be able to keep them down for at least twenty minutes so your body can absorb the medicine," the nurse said.

Kyle gave him a nasty look. "I would if I could, man." Then he looked to Emery. "Are you the doctor?"

"I'm a mycologist," she said. "I'm here to figure out exactly what you ate."

Emery noticed Kyle was in his early to mid-twenties, just like Brandon Hawthorne, and that he was slightly jaundiced, indicating decreased liver function on top of the GI symptoms. All in line with amatoxin poisoning, although there were plenty of more common things to rule out first.

"So you're, like, a mushroom poisoning expert?" he asked. "Am I gonna make it?"

Emery opened her mouth, but no words came. If this young kid really had eaten a destroying angel, the chances were no better than fifty-fifty. It was good he'd come into the ER while he was still experiencing gastrointestinal symptoms... still not great though.

Julia filled the silence just before it became awkward. "Dr. Ellison is one of the top mycologists in the state – if you ingested a toxic mushroom, she'll find out and let the doctors know so they can treat you."

That was Emery's cue to step back into the conversation. "I was told you brought a sample of the mushrooms you ate?"

"Yeah, it's there," Kyle said, pointing to a tray table where a glass casserole dish sat covered in foil. He looked too green to say much more, but unfortunately for him, Emery had questions and they couldn't wait.

"How long ago did you eat this?" she asked, peeking under the foil. Something with egg noodles and visible chunks of mushroom, cooked down too much to tell her anything by looks alone. There were a couple big scoops missing from the dish.

"I don't know... dinnertime," he groaned.

"And you made it yourself?"

He nodded, looking like he was going to be sick again.

"Where did you get the mushrooms?"

Emery turned around just fast enough to avoid watching the nurse raise the emesis basin to Kyle's mouth again, then felt very unprofessional for needing to avert her eyes. But hey, she was a lab geek, not a medical doctor. She caught Julia's gaze while they waited out this latest round of retching, and made a mental note that even in these circumstances, the detective was a drop-dead stunner.

Maybe even prettier for the fact that her ponytail was slightly mussed and her shirt wasn't as perfectly tucked in as it usually was.

"You're never going to keep down the anti-emetics," the nurse sighed. "We're going to have to try a sedative."

"Please, God, sedate me," Kyle complained. When Emery and Julia turned back to face him, his skin was clammy and his head was back against the pillow. The nurse had stepped out, presumably to retrieve the sedative.

"I'm sorry, Kyle, but where did you get the mushrooms?" Emery insisted.

He groaned loudly, more out of annoyance than pain, and said, "I foraged them. I guess I fucked up big-time."

"Sounds like you got here fast, though," she said.

"Early intervention comes with the best odds. I know you said you ate the mushrooms at dinner, but how long ago did your symptoms begin?"

"I don't know, three, four hours ago?" he said. "I tried to stick it out at home, thought I had food poisoning at first, but I couldn't stop throwing up, so I came in."

"We took one look at the color of his skin and started running all the tests we could do in-house," the nurse explained as he stepped back in. "His liver is shutting down."

"Well, it's good that you brought what you ate," Emery said. "I'm going to analyze this specimen right away."

She picked up the casserole dish, and Julia stepped closer to her. "I'll walk you out, if you don't mind."

Emery nodded, all too eager to extricate herself from the situation. They pushed through the curtain and went in the direction of the parking lot.

"By the time I got the call to come down here, someone already called the university for an antigen sample. I was hoping they'd send you," Julia said, and her hand brushed Emery's as they walked.

"Did your boss chew you out for being late coming back from lunch the other day?"

"Sure did," Julia said. "I deserved it though."

"I'm sorry for my part in it." Emery walked a little closer to her.

They got outside, the cool spring air refreshing after the stifling atmosphere inside. Julia's arm brushed

Emery's as they walked and she said, "I didn't want to ask in front of Kyle, but what are his real chances?"

"Best they could be if it really is amatoxin," Emery said. "He came in fast, and brought the casserole. Both the best things you can do."

"Which makes me more than a little suspicious," Julia answered.

"Oh?"

"He's acting like he knows exactly what he ate," Julia said. "I just don't know why. Hey, would it be against lab policy for me to come keep you company while you run your tests? They're knocking him out so there's nothing more for me to do here right now."

Emery's brow furrowed. "You want to? It's going to take a couple hours – mostly just making slides and staring into a microscope."

"I don't mind," Julia said. "If you don't."

There was that pesky smile again, completely inappropriate in this situation and yet Emery couldn't get rid of it. "I'd like that."

16
JULIA

The campus was lit up with security lights all around the parking lot and inside the biology building, but it felt eerily quiet at this hour. Julia parked her car right next to Emery's in the parking lot, then took her elbow when she offered it.

"Kinda spooky out here," she said.

Emery gave her a side-long smile that somehow made her feel marginally safer. "Are you scared of the dark, Detective Taylor?"

Not so much the dark itself, but who could be lurking in it, she thought. Would she ever quit looking over her shoulder everywhere she went?

But she wasn't going to say all that to Emery. Instead, she smiled and said, "Only as an excuse to get a little closer to you."

Emery unlocked the building with a thick brass key she pulled from her pocket, and led Julia up a flight of stairs then down a low-lit hallway to the lab.

"PPE on," she said as she handed Julia a pair of safety goggles and a mask. Then she donned a set of her own, as well as an apron and a pair of latex gloves.

Even covered in protective gear, with very little of her face showing, Emery still proved to be difficult to look away from. Julia watched in rapt attention as she went about picking little bits of mushroom out of the casserole and slicing them thin, then mounting them to slides and stuffing them down into test tubes. Julia stayed quiet so as not to disturb her.

Pipettes, test tubes, centrifuges... Julia recognized a few of Emery's tools from her college chemistry class, but mostly it was all just *science stuff* to her. Emery moved with confidence and skill, and it was hypnotizing watching her work.

Or maybe that was on account of the fact it was well past her bedtime and she could feel the weight of her eyelids the longer she sat there and watched.

Emery fed some of the sample mushrooms into a large machine along one wall, then studied the slides she'd made through a complex-looking microscope. At last, she stripped off her gloves and said, "Microscopic exam is inconclusive, as I pretty much knew it would be with the condition the sample was in. So now we wait."

"For what?"

"The mass spec to do its thing," she answered, pointing to the large *science machine* that she'd used earlier. "Could take up to an hour, depending on what it finds. Do you want to wait in my office? I could make us coffee."

Julia's body let out an exhausted scream for caffeine and she eagerly stripped off her goggles and mask. "That sounds heavenly."

Emery's office was down the hall a bit further. She turned on a desk lamp rather than the overhead light, which was cozy and nice, but maybe a little too sleep-inducing for the hour. Julia sank into a plush chair across from Emery's desk that looked like it hadn't been reupholstered since the seventies, but it was soft and well-kept.

In fact, everything in the office was decidedly midcentury modern.

"Your choice of furniture or the university's?" she asked while Emery went to a file cabinet against the wall that had a Keurig on top of it.

She turned and gave Julia a look that started something smoldering in her belly. "Why? Do you like it or hate it?"

Julia laughed. "I wouldn't choose it, but it seems to suit you."

"The desk came with the office," Emery said. "The chairs belonged to my dad. I have a lot of fond memories of sitting in them in his office when I was a kid, and when I got this job, he gifted them to me." She held up a small handful of coffee pods. "Breakfast blend, hazelnut or peanut butter fudge?"

Julia raised her eyebrows. "Peanut butter fudge coffee?"

"I like a variety," Emery said, "and I'll take that as a yes."

She turned her back to Julia, busying herself with the Keurig. That gave Julia ample opportunity to look around the rest of the room and use her detective skills to learn what she could about her new companion.

Neat and tidy, with everything in its place.

Still a comfortable room, not sterile-feeling at all.

But aside from the chairs and a single wall hanging, no personal effects either.

Julia went to the wall art, then grinned. "Is this one of your spider web... what did you call it?"

"Preservations," Emery said. "Yes. Actually, I picked one out from my collection that I think you'll like, but it's at my apartment because I wasn't expecting to see you tonight."

"Or this morning, as the case may be," Julia smirked. She turned her attention back to the framed spiderweb, its silks intricately woven and carefully captured. "It's beautiful."

"Not a weird hobby?" Emery asked.

Julia smiled. "Weird in a good way."

She went back to her chair and sat down, then noticed one more personal effect, a glass paperweight on the desk. She picked it up, scrutinizing it. Suspended within the glass – or maybe it was resin – was a tiny, complete organism. A little brown mushroom, of course, including the fibrous roots that you typically never saw because they were so fragile they'd break off if you tried to uproot them.

When Emery turned around, two cups of coffee in

hand, she saw the direction of Julia's gaze and said, "*Armillaria ostoyae.*"

"Bless you."

Emery smirked as she set down Julia's coffee. "It's a typical button mushroom, but what you're holding in your hand is actually a tiny piece of the largest single organism ever discovered. The rest of it would take up almost four square miles if you condensed it."

"And you stole a piece to hold your papers in place?" Julia teased.

"It was gifted to me," Emery explained, "by the scientists who discovered it. The rest of it is out in Oregon, and I don't really think it misses... itself."

"You don't *think?*" Julia couldn't help pressing Emery's buttons because every time she did it, she got to see those deep dimples in her cheeks. She returned the paperweight to the desk and lifted her coffee cup, and peanut butter fudge flooded her senses. "Oh wow, that is peanut butter coffee, all right."

"Well, when you put it that way it sounds gross," Emery laughed. She waited til Julia had a sip, then asked, "So?"

"I like it." She took another sip. "Mmm, I really do."

"I'll send you with a few K-cups for the precinct," Emery promised.

Julia laughed. "The police department has shit coffee, don't bother. We all go to the little coffee shop across the street when we need a hit of caffeine – I think we're the café's entire *raison d'être.*"

Emery took a drink from her own mug, then sat in the

chair beside Julia. She seemed to be enjoying it, the dynamic suddenly flipping from Julia being in charge to Emery taking the lead. "So, why did you want to come here? Just to spend time with me?"

Julia nibbled her lip. Dare she just come out with the truth like that?

"I figured it'd be a good idea to be here as soon as you had the lab results," she chickened out. "And I have some questions."

All of which was true. None of which required her to follow Emery to a closed university in the middle of the night and cozy up in her office.

"What are your questions?"

Okay... work first, play later.

Julia set down her coffee cup, growing serious. "The two cases *have* to be related, right? What are the odds?"

"It's possible that it's a coincidence," Emery said, "but if my lab results come back with *A. bisporigera,* I'll say that the probability that Hawthorne and Brogan consumed the same toxic mushroom three weeks apart in the same city with no connection between them is very low."

"Could it be environmental?" Julia asked. "Like how people get sick when they've been living in a house with black mold? Could Brandon have inhaled the spores?"

Emery shook her head. "Again, the odds are astronomical. When consumed orally, a very low dose of amatoxin can prove fatal, but it's a myth that you can get sick from mushrooms – any kind – simply by absorbing the toxin through your skin or inhaling it. It just doesn't work like that."

"So they both *had* to have ingested it." Julia sighed. "We just don't know the connection between them."

"How do you figure that out?" Emery asked.

"Well, we know Kyle ate it in a casserole, and based on his reaction, he seemed to know what made him sick, even if he was claiming it was accidental," Julia said.

"But you don't believe it was accidental," Emery said.

"Like you said, the chances that he accidentally poisoned himself and another man in the same city accidentally consumed or was dosed with the same poison three weeks before? Let's just say Kyle Brogan has suddenly become suspect number one in the Hawthorne case. I guess I'm just glad my number one theory is no longer accidental poisoning from a restaurant."

"Sounds like your job isn't all glamor and drama like they make it appear on TV," Emery said, then snorted. "Nobody ever accuses a mycologist of having a thrilling career."

"Oh, investigating is so much more paperwork than anyone expects," Julia laughed. "Whenever someone asks me what I do and I don't want to get into it, I just say data entry and it's not technically a lie."

"I say I study fungus," Emery answered. "Then all of a sudden I have an extra seat between me and whoever asked me the question."

"It can't be that bad," Julia shot back.

Emery smirked, her dimples making an appearance.

Heat radiated in Julia's body, and it wasn't because of the coffee.

"I can tell you one time when I *don't* make a point of mentioning my job," Emery said. "When I'm trying to flirt."

The smile fell from Julia's face – did that mean she wasn't flirting now? Was she reading this situation all wrong?

But then Emery hurried to add, "Present company excluded... it's pretty much impossible to avoid the topic when it's the only thing I have to tempt you with."

"Tempt me with?"

"To get your attention."

Julia squirmed in her seat, the warmth spreading through her. "You can have my attention whenever you want it."

17
EMERY

"Is that so?"

Emery couldn't help herself. She leaned forward in her chair. All the while, a little voice in her head asked, *What are you doing?*

But Julia leaned in too, and now they were mere inches from each other in the softly lit quiet of Emery's office.

"You bring women here often?" Julia asked.

"If you'll recall, you invited yourself."

Emery moved closer, and watched a muscle in Julia's neck flex as her breath caught in her throat. It was arresting, and she had a sudden strong urge to run her tongue along that line.

"I'm glad you let me come," the detective answered, her voice all breathy and soft. The subtext lingered in the air between them until Emery closed the gap.

She threaded her fingers through Julia's soft hair,

nudging the ponytail holder down for the first time since they met. The warm, earthy smell of her filled Emery's office, and she tilted Julia's chin up to meet her gaze.

"You're beautiful."

"So are you."

And then their mouths came together, tentative at first, exploring each other, testing limits.

Then the urgency took over. Julia stepped into Emery's embrace, their bodies coming together. Her face tipped up further, eagerly seeking her, and her mouth opened slightly, inviting Emery in.

In a matter of seconds, all the tension that had been building between them since that first day in the forest bubbled to the surface and then boiled over. Their tongues danced over each other and Emery thrilled at the feeling of Julia's hands roaming over her hips, grabbing onto her beltloops to keep her close.

"Touch me," she murmured against Julia's lips. "Like you did before."

She could feel Julia smiling right back at her. "When I tripped?"

"Yes." Too impatient to wait, Emery took Julia's hands in her own and planted her palms firmly against her chest.

They were warm and soft, and unlike the first time, they lingered there. Julia cupped and kneaded Emery's small breasts, making her nipples stand at attention and ache to be touched without all that pesky fabric in between them.

"Is that nice?" Julia asked, abandoned Emery's lips to kiss a trail down her neck, hands still teasing her breasts.

"So good."

"What else do you want?"

"You." Emery's brain was barely functioning – all she had left were single-syllable words. "All of you."

Never mind that they were in her office, with not so much as a couch to lie down on. Never mind that even though it was early in the morning, there was always the possibility of being caught.

Never mind that they'd just met last week.

Who was this new version of Dr. Emery Ellison?

Her fingers went to the buttons of Julia's cotton shirt, working them open as quickly as she could. She didn't just want Julia – she *needed* her. Like she never had with any other woman before.

"Take me," Julia whispered into her ear, sending a thrill down Emery's spine. Then she stepped back, hopped up on Emery's desk, and stared her down with a challenge in her eyes.

"Oh damn." Emery bit her lip.

"When you do that, your dimples pop."

"Yeah? You like my dimples?"

"I love them," Julia said, giving her an irresistibly sultry look. "Come here."

Emery obeyed. In that moment, she'd do any damn thing her detective asked of her, and she was pretty sure she would have the very first time they met, too.

"What is it about you?" she mused. "I can't stop thinking about you."

Then she stepped into the space between Julia's spread knees, grabbing her hips and pulling her to the edge of the desk. Julia let out a groan as her core made contact with Emery's hips, and she immediately started to grind against her. Fuck, that was going straight into Emery's long-term memory because that feeling was heaven.

"I haven't been able to stop thinking about you either," Julia said while Emery finished the job of unbuttoning her shirt. "I secretly hoped this would happen tonight."

Emery pulled Julia's shirt open and a fresh wave of desire coursed through her as she took in the modest white bra and the supple curves of Julia's breasts spilling over the cups.

"I didn't see this coming, but I'm so glad it did," Emery admitted before lowering her head to kiss the tops of Julia's breasts. Her skin was sweet and fresh-smelling, as if she'd come straight from a shower.

"I have a confession," Julia murmured as she ran her hands over Emery's hair, keeping her attention on her chest.

"Yes?" Emery looked up between Julia's breasts, taking a second to try to memorize the view.

Julia paused for a moment, conflict written on her face. "I didn't expect to meet anyone in Fox County so soon... but I've thought about you... about this."

Emery stood up. "Really?"

Julia nodded eagerly. "I couldn't help myself."

Emery's body pulsed with need, an ache beginning

between her legs. She tried to redirect the feeling, her hand sliding up Julia's thigh. She stroked her softly through her pants, feeling heat and wetness growing there, even through her layers.

"You couldn't help yourself what?" Emery teased, and as soon as Julia canted her hips in her direction, seeking more of her touch, she increased the pressure. "Did you touch yourself and imagine it was me?"

Julia bit down on her lip again, trying and failing to suppress a moan. "I did." Her big brown eyes flitted up to meet Emery's gaze. "Was that bad?"

Instead of answering, Emery brought her fingers to the button on Julia's pants. She popped it open, then slipped her hand inside. Her panties were soaked, her pussy already throbbing with need. Julia wrapped herself around Emery, her head going over Emery's shoulder as she clung to her.

"I only wish I'd been there," Emery said, "so you didn't have to pretend."

"Well, you're here now–"

She let out a gasp on that last word as Emery swiftly hooked Julia's panties aside and sank a finger into her wetness, then two.

"Oh fuck!" Julia groaned into her ear, immediately starting to ride Emery's hand. "Yes, right there. Oh my god..."

She really was close, the scent of her arousal filling Emery's head and making her dizzy with lust. Her palm was soaked after just a few thrusts, and she could feel Julia's muscles contracting against her fingers.

"More?" she asked, poising a third finger at Julia's entrance.

"Can you rub my clit too?"

Emery considered for a second. "Not with your pants on."

She yanked Julia off the desk, back on her feet, and Julia wasted no time in shoving her pants and her underwear down to her knees. "I'm close already. Kiss me," she said the moment she was bare, grabbing Emery by the collar of her shirt and pulling her in.

She would have liked a chance to glimpse the wetness she was responsible for, or better yet, taste the gorgeous, confident, slightly bossy woman in front of her. But Julia was shoving her tongue into Emery's mouth and reaching blindly for her hand, pawing it back between her legs. She was begging Emery for release, and damn if that wasn't the sexiest thing ever.

She plunged two fingers back into Julia's core, and used her thumb to drag some of that slickness up to her swollen clit, circling around and around and matching the motion of Julia's tongue in her mouth.

"Good?" she asked.

Julia used one foot to drag Emery's office chair closer and propped her foot up on it, opening herself wider for her. "More," was all she said. "Deeper."

Emery shivered, her own body throbbing with the most intense arousal she'd ever known. She'd do anything for this woman – now she was positive of that fact. And so she gave her more, plunged into her harder, fucked her with everything she had.

And just seconds later, Julia was coming loudly and almost violently against her hand. Her fingers dug into Emery's shoulders and her moans were most definitely carrying all the way down the hall to the empty lab, and her pussy spasmed hard, again and again over Emery's fingers. Julia bucked her hips, wringing every last drop of pleasure out of the moment, and at last collapsed back against the desk.

Emery just stood there, momentarily forgetting her own arousal as she drank the detective in.

Her hair was wild, her shirt flung open with one nipple starting to escape over the top of her bra cup. Her knees were wide, one leg still propped up on Emery's chair, and her pussy was swollen and dripping with the evidence of her desire.

Her desire for me, Emery thought, nakedly admiring the woman in front of her. *I did that.*

When she finally succeeded in dragging her eyes back up to Julia's face, she saw color in her cheeks and she watched as Julia brushed the wild strands back behind her ears.

"Wow," she said, reaching down to pull her pants up. "That got wild kind of fast."

"Too fast?" Emery asked.

"No," Julia answered, too casual. "Just right. Now let me return the favor–"

There was a beeping down the hall, and Julia's head wrenched toward the door. They hadn't even bothered to close it – anyone could have walked in and seen them, provided someone else was in the building.

"What's that?" she asked.

"Mass spec is done," Emery said with a sigh. "I need to go check the results."

18
JULIA

They went down the hall to the lab.

Julia followed in Emery's wake, her head swimming with what just happened. Not even twenty-four hours ago, she'd been panicked by the idea of her coworkers finding out her real name, her real story.

Thinking Fox County might only be a pit-stop on her flight from Samantha.

She was still afraid of that, and yet here she was begging Emery Ellison to fuck her in her office.

Damn if she hadn't needed that, though. She had barely even touched herself, even in a mechanical *just for stress relief* kind of way, since she left Michigan. Until Emery, she thought she wouldn't want another woman to touch her for a very long time.

But when she was around Emery, the desire came over her like a flash flood. Unexpected, maybe even dangerous.

When they got to the lab, Emery switched into

professional gear. She handed Julia her safety goggles and mask and donned her own protective gear, then went to the mass spectrometer to read the results.

"Well?" Julia asked, attempting to read over her shoulder even though the science speak meant nothing to her.

"*Amanita bisporigera*," Emery confirmed, "same as Brandon Hawthorne consumed."

"I'll call the hospital."

Her phone was still in Emery's office. Julia went down the hall to retrieve it, and when she was finished talking to the ER doc, she found Emery leaning in the doorway.

"They're going to start liver dialysis," Julia said.

"Good."

"Do you think we caught it soon enough this time?"

"I hope so," Emery said. She took a step toward Julia, who shouldered her bag and took a step away.

"I should really get going."

The feeling of Emery's body against hers had been just as incredible as she imagined it, but now that the high of her orgasm was gone, it just seemed foolish to keep going down this road. Get attached, get her heart smashed into pieces all over again? No thanks.

More importantly, there was the danger she could be putting Emery in if Sam *did* track her down only to find her with a new woman.

No, it was better for everyone if she kept her distance, pretended tonight's little indulgence hadn't happened.

"I need to take that casserole dish to our evidence

techs, see what they can find," she said by way of an excuse.

"Right," Emery said. She checked the time on her watch. "Well, it's past four – not sure if there's much point in going back to sleep now."

Julia smirked. "Early bird, huh?"

"The early bird finds the good mushrooms," Emery winked back.

19

EMERY

"*What* is going on with that look?"

"Hmm?" Emery looked up from the microscope where she was finally getting back around to the research project that had taken a backseat to all her new duties. Monica was staring at her. "What look?"

"You look like you're having the best damn day of your life, but as far as I can see, this is just an ordinary day and those are just ordinary spores you're looking at."

"They're *Armillaria ostoyae*," Emery explained. "I finally had a few days in a row without any community outreach on my schedule, so I'm excited to get back to my research. That's all."

"Bullshit."

Damn it. Why did best friends have to come with x-ray vision? Emery could get nothing past Monica, even on days when she was distracted with morning sickness.

"It's not bullshit, I *am* happy I have time for my research," she tried to insist.

"I know you are," Monica said, "but I know your 'happy nerd' face, and this isn't it. I can see that there's more to it. Besides, weren't you in here at like, four a.m. running tests for the hospital?"

"Three."

"Ugh. You should be falling asleep at your desk, not grinning like a fool."

Emery attempted to shrug off her friend's questions again, but Monica just kept staring at her, waiting for an answer. And suddenly, it erupted from her like a baking soda and vinegar volcano experiment.

"Okay, okay, you know that detective I've been consulting for?"

"I knew it!"

"You knew what?"

"I knew it had to do with her," Monica said, self-satisfaction practically vibrating off her. "So, what about her? Did you hook up?" A split second later, she gasped, reading the truth on Emery's face. "You did!"

"She was at the hospital last night when I showed up," Emery explained. "She came back to the lab with me while I ran the tests."

Scandal broke across Monica's face and she was practically screaming now. "You hooked up with her *here*?"

"Shh!" Emery considered lying, but there was no way Monica would buy it. "In my office. It was amazing, and I can't stop thinking about her."

"No shit, she's written all over your face. I am so jealous."

Emery raised an eyebrow. "You haven't even met her, and I didn't think you were into women."

"No, that you hooked up in the office! Bucket list item, for sure," Monica said.

"Since when?"

"Since my pregnancy hormones have started making me want to fuck twenty-four, seven," she said. "Plus I'm constantly overheating, and I bet this stainless steel would feel nice on my back."

Emery lifted her hands off the counter. "Promise me you've never been naked in the lab."

Monica laughed. "Don't worry, Dean is not adventurous enough to indulge me... not that I haven't tried."

"Good for Dean," Emery said, praising Monica's husband.

Monica gave her a cross look. "Hypocrite. Why do you get to do it and I don't?"

"Well, for one thing, it was not premeditated," Emery said. "And for another, at least we kept our bodily fluids confined to my office. I would never have sex in a lab."

She put her eye down to the microscope again and Monica snorted. "Oh, live a little."

The two of them worked for a while, side by side, on their own separate projects. Then Monica asked if Emery was planning to ask Julia out properly.

"I know you're usually a lone-wolf type, but it seems like there's something special about this girl," she added.

Emery lifted her head from her microscope again.

"You can tell that from the second-hand stories I've told you about her?"

"I can tell from how you've changed since you met her. You're more confident, more comfortable in your own skin."

She thought for a minute, then let out a dreamy little sigh that just didn't want to stay in. "Yeah, she is special."

"Then call her."

"I will. At lunch."

She looked down at her work again, and Monica – still full of that self-satisfaction – said, "Good. You deserve love, Em."

20
JULIA

*J*ulia didn't answer when Emery called her that afternoon, and she didn't reply to the text message that came in that evening either.

She wanted to – very badly. And it would be the polite thing to do after the woman completely and utterly wrecked her with one of the best orgasms of her life. Emery was constantly on her mind.

But Julia wasn't in a good place right now – not good enough to be dating someone new. Not when she was looking for Samantha around every corner and flinching at every unidentified noise in her apartment at night.

Maybe after a good, long stint in therapy.

Maybe when she knew Sam was gone for good – if that was even possible. It felt like she was waiting for the other shoe to drop, and as much as she liked Emery, it wasn't fair to drag her into the muck too.

So Julia kept her head down and focused on the case

for the next couple of days. She tried unsuccessfully to find family members for Kyle Brody – he didn't have an emergency contact listed in his files and had refused the hospital's offer to reach out to someone. Weird, but not evidence that he was a killer.

Julia also recruited Ariel to go with her to check out Kyle's apartment, since Tom and Renee were now busy with the skeleton-in-the-tree case.

"What are we hoping to find, a dartboard with Brandon Hawthorne's face on it?" Ariel asked as they explored the place.

"That would certainly help," Julia said with a smirk. "Look for mushroom foraging books, medical books, a computer we can search..."

She trailed off as she opened Kyle's refrigerator.

"Huh."

"What?" Ariel asked.

"Two take-out containers, a half-drunk gallon of milk, and mustard that expired last year," Julia inventoried. "Not exactly the fridge of a guy who would whip himself up a casserole."

Ariel joined her in the kitchen, opening cupboards. "He only has one pot – a chef's kitchen this is not."

The whole apartment was messy but not quite slovenly, and it didn't look like Kyle got many visitors. He definitely didn't cook for himself. She took pictures of everything, and they moved on to the bedroom. Drool-stained pillowcase, box of tissues at the bedside, mattress and TV both sitting directly on the floor.

If Brandon Hawthorne's apartment was a picture of a

man who'd been sick recently but generally had his life together, Kyle Brody's said the opposite. Julia could practically smell the depression – a scent akin to the pile of unwashed laundry accumulating in the bottom of the closet.

"Okay, I think I've seen enough," she said. "I need to go talk to this guy again."

Kyle Brody was sitting up in his hospital bed when Julia arrived.

He'd been moved to the intensive care unit to begin his liver dialysis, but at least he was no longer trying to regurgitate his own internal organs. He looked exhausted, and he was hooked up to a number of tubes and beeping machines, but he also looked relieved.

"Do you know what you ate, Mr. Brody?" Julia asked as she helped herself to a seat next to his bed.

"Destroying angel," he said. "Didn't quite finish the job though, did it?"

"Is that what you wanted?" Julia asked.

"To kill myself? No!" Kyle hissed. "Far from it."

"Your doctor says you're not out of the woods yet." Although the digestive symptoms had abated in the time she'd been at the lab with Emery, Kyle's liver and kidneys were still battling for survival. He'd likely recover, but maybe not without multiple organ transplants.

"And you can't tell me where you foraged that mushroom?" she pressed.

"Not specifically, other than from the woods around my apartment," Kyle said, his head flopping limply against his pillow. "Sorry."

"Are you feeling okay?" Julia asked, eyeing the call button dangling over the rail of his bed.

"Just tired." His eyes were closed and his skin was looking clammy. She should let him rest... but a man was dead and even though she couldn't make the connection between them, Julia knew there was one. He *had* to answer her questions, for the sake of Brandon's family.

Time to put the pressure on.

"How long are you going to keep pretending you made that casserole, Mr. Brody?"

His eyes fluttered open. "What?"

"I went to your apartment," she said. "I know you're not a cook."

"Oh, you know me?"

"I know you have one pot in your kitchen and it's barely big enough to make a box of Kraft Mac n' Cheese."

He shot her an annoyed look. "On second thought, I am feeling pretty sick... you better let me rest."

"Just a few more questions," Julia said, the compassion gone from her voice. "Who did you piss off?"

"Excuse me?"

"A friend of Brandon Hawthorne, maybe?"

She studied him closely, lucky that he was actually choosing to look her in the eyes now. There was no flicker of recognition, and he shook his head.

"That name supposed to mean something to me?"

"I thought it might," she said.

"Nope," Kyle said, his head flopping back on the pillow. He was starting to look pale and genuinely tired, not just annoyed.

"Maybe you have a mutual acquaintance. Whoever made you that casserole?"

"I don't know the guy," he gritted out. "And I told you, I made that casserole."

"So you were trying to kill yourself," Julia insisted. She didn't buy his story – the guy's kitchen told the tale of someone who could barely boil water – but she'd humor him for the moment.

"No, it was an accident." He was looking at the ceiling as he talked. The machines he was hooked up to were noisier now, and Julia knew if Tom were here he'd make her stop. "God, I could think of a thousand less painful ways to off myself if I wanted to."

A nurse came in and checked his vitals, and the machines calmed down. Julia watched the nurse draw his blood from an IV in the back of his hand. He didn't seem to be on any friendlier terms with the hospital staff than he was with her.

"I'll be back in an hour," the nurse said on her way out.

"Can't wait," Kyle grimaced. He turned back to Julia. "Hourly blood draws to make sure my kidneys and liver don't give up on me."

Julia hoped they didn't – for his sake and because she needed more time with him. He obviously wasn't going to tell her the truth today.

"I'll let you rest," she said. "One more thing before I go."

"Yeah?"

"Why didn't you ask the hospital to notify an emergency contact that you're here?"

"I don't *have* an emergency contact, okay?" It was the first time that an emotion other than anger rose to the surface, and Julia thought she heard his voice crack. "I have no one. My parents are dead, I'm an only child, it's just me."

Empathy twisted in Julia's chest in spite of herself.

She believed Kyle had something to do with Brandon's death. Otherwise, why lie about the casserole?

And yet, part of her felt bad for him.

She hesitated, then went over to the tray table beside his bed and poured him a cup of water because no one had thought to do it yet. She handed it to him and dropped a straw into the cup. He started drinking without a thanks, and she said, "I'll be in contact, Mr. Brody. Feel better."

21
EMERY

By the end of the work week, Emery was getting pretty despondent over Julia's complete lack of communication.

Emery had tried texting her a couple of times, until it felt like the string of unanswered messages was starting to look needy. She was trying to resign herself to the fact that she'd been ghosted, but at lunch on Friday, Monica was determined to get Emery to call her again.

"She's probably just busy," she said. "She's a detective working a homicide case, and she just moved into a new town. I bet her routine's all screwed up and she just forgot to answer your texts."

"We had great chemistry and we really clicked, we had sex and now she's done with me," Emery said, trying to feel as nonchalant as her words implied.

"She is not done with you," Monica insisted. "You *do* have great chemistry. You went to lunch together and couldn't stop talking about how intriguing she is. That's not hit it and quit it behavior. *Call her.*"

So Emery did, against her better judgment, and she was sent to voicemail.

"What do I do?" she asked Monica.

"Leave a message," Monica said, rolling her eyes like it was the most obvious answer in the world.

Emery's heart climbed into her throat, threatening to cut off her words. Nobody liked talking on the phone anymore, and that included leaving voicemails. She hadn't left one for a non-work-related reason in she couldn't remember how long – what the hell was she supposed to say?

Hey, I know you didn't answer any of my texts, which you definitely would have done if you actually wanted to talk to me. So here I am, barging into your voicemail, making a pest of myself.

The longer she tried to think of something to say, the more dead air got recorded and the more awkward the whole message became.

She was just about to hang up when Monica snatched the phone out of her hand. "Hey, this is a message on behalf of Emery Ellison. She had fun in the lab on Sunday night and she wants to know when you're free to do it again. Bye!" She hung up, then handed the phone back to Emery. "Was that so hard?"

"Um, *yeah*. Excruciating. Thank you."

Emery figured that was the end of Julia – unless something came up with the case. She tried to put her out of her head, but just as she was walking into her apartment that night, Julia called her back.

Emery saw the caller ID on her smartwatch and immediately started juggling her messenger bag and coat. She ended up throwing all of it on the floor and answering the call right there on her watch because she was scared she wouldn't get another chance.

"Hello?"

"You sound out of breath – is this a bad time?" Julia asked.

"No," Emery said, doing her best to force the wind back into her lungs without it being audible through the speaker. "What's up?"

"Well, first of all, I'm really sorry I ghosted you."

"Oh, no, you didn't ghost me. It's cool."

See, Monica? She totally ghosted me. Emery could practically hear herself having that conversation at lunch on Monday.

"Yes, I did," Julia insisted, her tone apologetic. "What we did in your office kind of spooked me."

"Did I do something wrong?"

"No. God, no, you were amazing." Julia chuckled and it brought a satisfied smirk onto Emery's face. "Without getting into far more details than you need to hear over the phone, I have some baggage and I got nervous. I should have told you but instead I stuck my head in the sand. I'm sorry."

"No need to apologize." It was actually a relief to hear that Emery hadn't found some unique and creative way to fuck things up with Julia, that she hadn't somehow driven her away.

"I'm glad you called me," Julia said. "Or... who was that?"

Emery chuckled. "My best friend Monica. She was excited to play wing-woman."

"She's good at it," Julia said. There was a little silence, during which Emery started to think about what it felt like to have Julia pressed up against her desk... what it might feel like to bend her over one of the lab tables and finger her from behind...

Despite what she'd told Monica about how many different lab safety violations that would entail, she was secretly warming up to the idea.

"Anyway," Julia said, "I feel bad for how I treated you and I'd like to make it up to you. Can I take you out to dinner or something?"

Emery opened her mouth to tell Julia that wasn't necessary, that all had been forgiven, then paused.

What would Monica do?

"I'd like that," she said, "but rather than going out, why don't you come over to my place? We can open a bottle of wine, maybe pick up where we left off when the mass spec interrupted us."

"Your place?" Julia asked.

"Yeah, I can finally give you that web art I promised you."

There were a few seconds of silence on the line, during which Emery started to question what she'd just proposed. Was it stupid to be so forward when she was just resigning herself to never hearing from Julia again?

But then she said, "Text me the address. I'll be there in an hour."

Emery hung up the phone with the biggest smile on her face. First step, text Monica to tell her what a devilish, wonderful influence she was. Step two, pick up all the work stuff she just dumped all over the floor.

And step three, go let the wine breathe.

Pretty much exactly an hour later, Emery's intercom buzzed and she let Julia up to her apartment. She met her on the stairwell, and took the cloth shopping bag that Julia had looped over one arm.

"I brought 'sorry I'm a dick for ghosting you' cheese and crackers," she said.

"Is that what cheese and crackers means?" Emery asked. "I'm so out of the loop on social etiquette."

They went inside and Emery set the bag down on her kitchen counter. Julia followed her into the room, and it was a tight squeeze in the small kitchen. When Emery brushed by her on her way to grab a serving plate and some wine glasses, she inhaled Julia's sweet, fresh perfume. When Julia chose that exact moment to turn around, meeting her gaze all of ten inches from each other, well, Emery was a goner.

She abandoned her quest for dinnerware and planted both hands on the edge of the counter at Julia's hips. She leaned forward, indulging in her delicious scent and the swish of her ponytail as she said right against Julia's ear, "I missed you."

She was rewarded with the press of Julia's body against her own. Her hands on Emery's hips. Her breath warm and inviting on her neck as she answered, "I missed you too."

And then they were kissing, hot and heavy just like in Emery's office.

It seemed that they both had incredible self-control when they needed it, but whenever either one of them broke the seal, all bets were off.

Soon, Emery had Julia hoisted up on the countertop, thighs squeezing Emery's hips. She had one hand tangled in Julia's hair and the other wrapped around her, holding her tight. She tasted like heaven, and Emery craved more of her, ached to lay this woman down in her bed and worship her like she deserved.

A quickie was great when it was the only option. But now they had the time to savor each other.

"You feel so good," she groaned as she scooted Julia's hips closer to the edge of the counter, enjoying the way Julia's body fit against her own.

"So do you," Julia murmured, her hands reaching down to grab Emery's ass and her legs hooking around the backs of her thighs.

"I want you."

"I want you too... wait."

Suddenly, Julia's hands were on Emery's chest, but

not in the way she wanted. She was pushing her back, making space between them.

"What's wrong?"

There was a storm behind Julia's eyes. "We should talk first. About why I got scared after Sunday morning."

"Is everything okay?"

"Yes... sort of..." Julia sighed. "I don't know how to explain it, and I'm afraid you'll hate me."

"I don't think that's possible," Emery said, stepping back and holding out her hand. "But let's have that glass of wine and you can tell me what's going on."

Julia took her hand. It was a drop of about six inches to the floor, but she smiled at the chivalry, which Emery took as a good sign. Whatever she had to say couldn't be that serious, right?

"Do you want the cheese and crackers?"

"Maybe later," Julia said.

So Emery grabbed a couple wine glasses and the bottle from the counter, and led Julia into the living room. Emery poured them each a glass and set the bottle down on the coffee table.

"I like your apartment – it's very cozy. Is that your spiderweb art?" Julia gestured to a couple of baroque-style frames on the wall.

"Yeah, this is the one I had in mind for you," Emery said, leading her over to an intricate web in a gilt oval frame. "But you can pick out whichever one you want if you like a different one."

"I love this one," Julia said. "And I like that you picked it for me."

Emery pulled it off the wall and set it on the kitchen counter beside Julia's purse so she'd remember to take it with her when she left. When she turned back around, she found Julia staring pensively into her wine glass, looking worried.

Emery came over and put a hand on top of Julia's. "You can talk to me. I promise there's nothing you can say that will make me hate you."

Julia downed a big gulp of wine, then turned to face her. "You can't promise that. You don't even know me."

"I haven't known you long, but I do think I know you."

"Don't be so sure," she said. "My name isn't even Julia Taylor."

22
JULIA

*E*mery's eyes subtly widened, and then she made an effort to narrow them so as not to look shocked. Julia's heart beat faster.

"It's not?" She let out a chuckle to try to lighten the mood. "What are you, an assassin? My opponent at the state mycological society must be taking the annual elections more seriously than usual."

Julia couldn't help laughing. She sputtered, trying not to spit the wine she'd been drinking.

"So you're *not* here to kill me for being too cool and knowledgeable during my lecture at the last conference?"

"I wouldn't announce it if I was," Julia shot back, grateful for the distraction. It was like Emery had pulled the tension relief valve and all the pressure building up in her came out at last. "But no, I'm not here to kill you and I'm not an assassin. I'm... well, not in actual witness protection, but it's kind of like that."

She sighed, then told Emery about Sam.

About how when they started dating, she'd seemed perfectly normal. And then that veneer had quickly cracked, Sam's jealous and possessive side coming to the surface with frightening regularity.

"I'm not naive – I'm a cop," Julia said. "I knew it was only going to get worse, so I cut ties, or tried to."

Samantha had only gotten clingier and scarier after Julia broke up with her. It had been a short relationship, but in Sam's head, it was everything, and Julia had ballooned in her mind into an ideal girlfriend that the real-world version could never live up to.

"I tried everything from stern warnings to a restraining order, and I even showed her picture to all my coworkers and family members in case she showed up where she wasn't welcome," she explained, "but none of it fazed her. She just didn't care, and she said she'd do anything to win me back. Including calling my old chief and making up lies, trying to get me fired because she thought I broke up with her because I was too busy with my job."

"That sounds awful, I'm sorry you had to go through it," Emery said. "And I'm sorry I sent you so many messages last week – that must have freaked you out."

"So many?" Julia wrinkled her brow. "I counted three. You should have seen how Sam used to blow up my phone... but I do appreciate that you worried about that."

"So what happened? Is she in prison for stalking you?"

"I wish." Julia took a deep breath. "There's a pretty

big correlation between intimate partner stalking and domestic violence. I was alone in my apartment back in Michigan one night when a rock crashed through my front window. That was it, no one tried to come in, but I know it was her and I took it as a warning. If she was willing to do something like that, I wasn't going to wait around for her to violate the restraining order so I could call the cops. I got the hell out of Dodge, and changed my name so she couldn't follow me."

I hope.

She was just about to go for her glass of wine again – feeling ready to down the whole thing – when Emery threw her arms around her and held her tight.

It felt good, firm and comforting. It instantly relaxed her even though her mind had been racing only moments before.

"I'm so sorry you had to go through that," Emery said into the hug. "And I'm so proud of you for looking out for yourself. Not everyone is strong enough to do that."

Tears threatened at the edges of Julia's eyelids but she blinked them back. When Emery released her from the hug, she drew another deep breath to clear her head. "Thank you. I still get freaked out sometimes in my new apartment, thinking I heard something on the street, or saw a shadow cross my bedroom window."

"I'd be jumping at shadows too if I went through that – anyone would."

"I'm a detective, though," Julia said. "I'm supposed to be... I don't know, better prepared."

"Says who?"

Julia didn't have an answer for that.

After a moment's hesitation, Emery added, "So... can I ask you what your real name is? Or is that a faux pas?"

"It's Frances Martin. Julia is my middle name," she said, then laughed. "I always hated Frances anyway, so I guess one good thing came of this."

"I like Frances," Emery said. "It's unique, like you."

"Frannie," Julia said, sticking out her tongue. "Or Fanny, as I got called as a kid."

"Well, I'll call you whatever you want me to," Emery said.

"Julia, please," she answered. "I had to tell Chief Wilson about my name change during my interview, and he would have found it during a background check anyway. But no one else here knows. Even to my detriment – one of my coworkers, Renee, knows something's up with me and she's so suspicious. But I can't get over this fear that Sam's going to find me the minute my old and new names get linked."

"But you trusted me," Emery said, pride evident on her face.

"I had to," Julia said. "Or this was never going to work out."

"This?"

"Us."

"Well, I'm glad you felt you could. My lips are sealed," Emery promised. "I won't tell a soul. And there's another bit of good news."

"What?"

"I can assure you that I don't hate you," she

answered. "In fact, I have an even higher opinion of you now than before you told me, because despite what you may think, the whole ordeal proves what a strong, incredible woman you are. And we can go as slowly as you want."

"Right now, I don't feel like going slow at all," Julia said, coy at first, but soon she was straddling Emery's lap, their wine forgotten once again.

The two of them ended up naked in Emery's bed, a platter full of cheese and crackers in between them. They'd made love, got famished and ventured to the kitchen for a snack, and then fucked again right there on the kitchen floor before eventually making their way back to the bedroom.

It was such a relief for Julia to have one more person in her life who knew her secret, who she didn't have to continually hide things from or worry that she'd forget to answer to her new name. Even more importantly, now she had an ally here in Fox County, a friend... certainly a lover, but maybe even more than that?

If she was ready for more...

She wasn't so sure about that, but it seemed that Emery was eager and willing, should it turn out that she was.

For now, she was just enjoying a creamy slice of smoked gouda on top of a rosemary cracker, trying not to get crumbs in bed and absently rubbing her foot against Emery's leg beneath the sheets.

"This is nice, right?" Emery asked.

She wasn't eating. She was simply propped up on her elbows, her dark brown nipples peeking out from the top of the sheet, her eyes on Julia.

"It is," Julia agreed, then shot Emery a sidelong glance. Her thoughts had taken a turn, and now she had something new on her mind. Emery read it on her face and she quickly moved the cheese and crackers off the bed.

Julia had Emery pinned against the headboard, hands gripping the bedposts while Julia thrust her fingers inside her... when the phone rang.

She nearly missed it. It was tucked into the pocket of her pants, which had been abandoned in the living room. If it'd been on vibrate, then nothing would have stopped her from relishing the blissed-out expression on Emery's face as Julia made her come just as hard as she had earlier.

But damn it, once she heard it, she couldn't ignore it.

"That's my work ringer," she apologized, hand stilling between Emery's thighs.

Anguish cut across Emery's features, but she nodded. "It's okay, duty calls."

Julia reluctantly climbed off the bed, sparing just one more moment to notice the fact that Emery wasn't stopping, even if Julia had to. She reached into her dresser drawer, pulled out a small vibrator, and lay back down on the bed.

"You're going to finish without me?" Julia pouted.

"Hurry back," Emery teased. "Maybe you can finish me off."

The vibrator buzzed to life and Julia had never felt more jealous of an inanimate object as she watched it disappear between Emery's thighs.

Then she forced the thought from her head as she sprinted through the apartment and snatched up her phone. The call had gone to voicemail, but she saw it was an FCPD number, just as she'd expected.

Rather than waste time listening to the voicemail, she just called back.

"Hey, it's Lena. You busy?" Detective Wolf asked asked as the call connected.

Julia looked down at her free hand, still slick with Emery's arousal. Fuuuck, she wanted to be back in that bedroom. She wanted to throw that damn vibrator out the window for daring to finish a job that she couldn't.

At least not this time.

She turned on the kitchen sink to wash her hands and ignored Lena's question, instead asking, "What's up?"

"I'm on third shift today and there's not much going on," she said. "I know you already checked social media for connections between your two mushroom poisonings, but I figured you might not have thought to check Nextdoor since you're not on social media and you probably don't have access to this area since you just moved–"

"Lena." She was rambling, and Julia was trying her best not to sound like someone who'd just gotten torn from between a gorgeous woman's thighs and was displeased about that.

"I found a connection," Lena said.

Damn, way to bury the lede! Julia felt *slightly* less guilty about leaving Emery to her own devices now. "Don't leave me hanging, what is it?"

"Nick Wilkins."

"Brandon's best friend? We cleared him."

"Up until a month ago, he lived in the same apartment building as Kyle Brody," Lena explained. "What do you think? That's too big a coincidence to be nothing."

Julia agreed, but she liked to think she could read people pretty well. She'd never gotten a bad feeling from Nick the whole time they were in the woods together, or when she questioned him with Tom. Was he involved after all?

As the sole link between Kyle Brody and Brandon Hawthorne, there had to be *something* she wasn't seeing about this kid.

"Thanks, Wolf, I'll take it from here," Julia said, and when she hung up the phone, she found Emery standing in the kitchen doorway, a sheet wrapped around her, shoulders glistening with perspiration.

"You have to go?"

"I'm really sorry," Julia said. "Hazard of the job."

"Well, you missed your chance to finish me off," Emery said, then came closer, murmuring against Julia's ear, "If it's any consolation, I came fast because you already had me really close to the edge."

"That does help, yes," Julia smiled. "But next time, I'm not giving up my place to a hunk of plastic."

"Hey, that hunk of plastic has been my number one for a long time," Emery teased. "Very reliable, always available, doesn't leave cracker crumbs in my bed."

Julia laughed. "You're the one who brought the cheese and crackers to bed." She stole a kiss, then added, "Maybe next time we can make it a three-way if your little plastic friend means so much to you."

"I'd rather just have you," Emery answered.

23
EMERY

The first Monday of the month was everyone in the mycology department's least favorite – everyone except Glen, that was. He loved it because it was faculty meeting day, the only day of the month when he got the full and undivided attention of each and every one of his employees. And he had the opportunity to delegate, nitpick and micromanage to his heart's content.

"Think I can fake morning sickness to get out of this?" Monica whispered as she and Emery found their customary seats at the side of the classroom they used for meetings.

"Don't abandon me," Emery shot back a warning glare.

"If he asks me to recite the grades of every single one of my students again, I'll have no choice," Monica answered.

The first half-hour of the meeting was simply Glen enjoying the sound of his own voice. He went over the things that everyone in the department was already fully aware of thanks to the modern miracle of email, and everyone did their best to look like they were paying attention. Emery was blissfully envisioning the curves of Julia's body and the way her skin tasted beneath Emery's tongue... she was content to zone out and let Glen ramble.

Then they all went around the room discussing their plans and challenges for the month. There were only five full-time faculty members, split evenly between research and teaching roles, but there were another half-dozen adjunct instructors who also had to stand and deliver at these meetings. Monica talked about some upcoming fieldwork she was planning for her upperclassmen, and thankfully Glen wasn't interested in their individual grades this time.

"Dr. Ellison?" he asked next.

She made a conscious effort not to slump down in her chair. She was fully expecting him to make her report on the debacle that had been Tarzan, err, Mason and his mother.

Instead, he said, "I hear you've had an eventful time working with the police lately."

Emery relaxed, a smile coming involuntarily to her lips as a certain ponytailed detective flashed in her mind's eye yet again. "Yes, I have."

She told everyone about the two amatoxin cases – or what she was permitted to say, considering the investigations were ongoing. They listened with genuine interest, and Glen nodded approvingly.

"You seem to be coming into your own, Dr. Ellison," he said at the end of her report. "Perhaps I won't be putting up a job posting to fill the community liaison position for next year after all."

A statement like that a couple months ago would have sent her practically under her desk with fear. Now, though, when Glen moved on to the next person and Monica leaned in to ask, "How do you feel about that?" she was surprised to find she didn't feel half bad.

"It'd look good on my resume," she said with a shrug.

Monica elbowed her. "More chances to work with the sexy detective too."

The meeting let out a short while later and everyone fled the classroom the same way students did at the end of a long lecture.

"Lunch?" Monica asked.

"We ate just before the meeting," Emery reminded her.

Monica just shrugged. "Baby's hungry again."

Emery's phone started to ring and she asked Monica to wait while she dug it out of her pocket. *Fox County Police Department* was on the screen, and Emery recognized Julia's extension.

Monica looked over her shoulder and said with a wry smile, "Guess I'm going to second lunch on my own."

"She's calling from her desk, that must mean it's business," Emery said, waving as she stepped away to take the call. "Hey, babe."

Okay, so she wasn't capable of being *fully* in professional mode whenever she was around Julia.

"Hi, are you busy?"

"Just finished a meeting," she said. "What's going on?"

"The hospital called," Julia answered. "Kyle Brody's getting sicker."

"His liver function?"

He'd been on dialysis and the transplant list since Emery confirmed the presence of amatoxin, which had given him the best chance of recovery. But with destroying angels, nothing was for certain.

But then Julia said, "No, back to vomiting and diarrhea."

Emery's brow furrowed deeply. "That shouldn't happen."

"I know," Julia answered. "You told me that GI symptoms happen in the first seventy-two hours, and the doctors I've spoken to have said the same thing. It's been over a week since Kyle last had those problems."

"Could he have a stomach bug from being in the hospital?" Emery wondered.

"I just got done talking to the doctor and she says he's got the *exact* same symptoms he came in with."

"She thinks he was exposed again," Emery concluded.

"Yep. Does that mean he ate more mushrooms?"

"I can't think of any other reason," she said. "If his new symptoms are due to amatoxin, there had to have been a second exposure."

24
JULIA

"What's he doing, dosing himself from his hospital bed?" Tom asked.

He and Julia were in his SUV again, en route to the hospital to see what kind of condition Kyle Brody was in.

"He doesn't seem like he's been well enough to do that," Julia said. "And he would have had to bring a second dose to the hospital with him."

"Or else someone brought it to him."

"Someone who was trying to help him commit suicide?" Julia asked. "What, out of guilt over what happened to Brandon Hawthorne?"

Tom just shook his head. "That or someone who has an ax to grind, a motivation we're not seeing to poison both men."

"And Kyle twice – he must have really pissed them off. Nick Wilkins is the only solid connection we have between them," she reminded him. "Same apartment building, but separate wings, separate floors."

She'd talked to him again after Lena called to tell her about the connection, but he'd seemed truthful when he said he didn't know Kyle.

"Besides, why would he poison his best friend?"

"Sometimes the people we're closest to hold the deepest grudges."

Tom parked in the hospital deck and they went to the ICU, where Kyle had been transferred once again after spending about a week in a less intensive department. When they arrived, a uniformed police officer was standing guard outside Kyle's door.

Julia asked the officer, "Any trouble?"

"Only been here twenty minutes, but I haven't seen anyone but medical staff."

Julia and Tom went into the room, where Dr. Nasir was checking Kyle's vitals. His face was a clammy yellow and his eyes were closed. The doctor explained, "He fell asleep just a couple minutes ago. I don't know if I'd wake him if I were you – he just stopped retching."

"Lovely," Tom said with a grimace.

"Maybe we should step out and talk with you instead," Julia suggested. "We can give Kyle a little time to recover."

When the doctor was finished with her work, the three of them went out to the nurses' station. She took a couple minutes to chart what she'd done for Kyle then turned her attention to the detectives.

"How long ago did his new GI symptoms start?" Julia asked.

"About twelve hours," Dr. Nasir said. "We can

control them pretty well with medication now that we know what we're dealing with, but that's only treating the symptoms – not the cause."

"And from what my mycology expert tells me, the cause can't be anything but repeat exposure," Julia said.

"Which means he either dosed himself, or someone poisoned him," Tom added. "Please tell me the hospital keeps meticulous visitor logs."

Dr. Nasir pursed her lips. "Not on this floor, but it wouldn't do you much good in this case anyway."

"Why's that?" Julia asked.

"He hasn't had any visitors," she said. "Not here in the ICU, and not in the whole time since he's been admitted.

"He's been here for almost two weeks," Julia objected. "I know he didn't want any emergency contact notified, but he hasn't reached out to *anybody* in that time? Not a single visitor?"

"Nobody," Dr. Nasir shook her head.

"Pretty unusual," Tom grunted. "What's the chances someone came to see him and nobody noticed?"

It was a good question – if your goal was to poison someone, the last thing you'd want was a bunch of people who could recognize your face.

"Unlikely," Dr. Nasir said. "Especially in the ICU, where there's staff around at all times checking on patients. But if you talk to the IT department, I'm sure someone can give you access to the hospital's security footage."

She pointed to a couple of domed cameras positioned

in the ceiling around the ICU. There were at least five of them, and one of them had a pretty good angle on Kyle's room. Hopefully there was another one near his last room too.

"We'll do that," Julia said.

An alarm started going off in a room at the other end of the ICU and a couple nurses went rushing past, one of them beckoning to the doc.

"Duty calls," Dr. Nasir said, and just like that, Tom and Julia were alone at the nurses' station.

Julia reached over the counter and picked up the tablet. It was still open to Kyle's chart, and she did her best to click around and read it, even though she was unfamiliar with the software, not to mention the medical terminology.

"Anything useful?" Tom asked.

"Nothing we don't already know." She set the tablet down and they poked their heads back into Kyle's room. "Do we want to wake him?"

"Not if he's going to be so busy puking he can't answer our questions," Tom said. "Let him rest. We'll work other angles and circle back."

If we get the chance, Julia thought. Emery had told her a lot about how amatoxin works in the body, and none of it was pretty. Kyle was lucky to survive his first brush with the toxin. With his organs already damaged and his body worn down from the fight, he might not win his second battle with it.

They went back to the police station, stopping in the evidence processing department to drop off a bag full of personal effects that they'd collected from Kyle's room. When he thought Julia was busy, Tom went over to a man bent over a microscope and gently swatted his ass, which took Julia by surprise. She stifled a laugh as she watched the man turn around and grin when he saw Tom. They shared a brief kiss, then Tom came over to meet Julia by the door.

"Sexually harassing the evidence techs?" she guessed.

"That's Christopher," Tom said. "My partner."

She smirked. "Yeah, I hoped so. That was pretty cute, you know. I think you're more of a softie than you like to let on."

"I don't know what you're talking about," he said.

"You have a reputation for matchmaking," Julia said as they made their way toward the elevator. "I've only been here a few weeks and I already know how many couples you've set up."

"Well, I hear things too, and it sounds like you're doing just fine for yourself when it comes to the mycologist."

Julia turned red at the suggestion, partly embarrassed and partly just struggling to figure out how she felt about the whole thing. Her feelings for Emery were clear, and she didn't want to put her life on hold just because her ex deserved a Danger sign hung around her neck at all times.

But every time Julia thought about the danger she was putting Emery in, a stone of guilt settled in her gut. It wasn't a good idea – not with Samantha still out there, very possibly still a threat.

"Let's grab coffee for whoever's around before we head back," she said, just to change the subject. Also, strategery. She had a favor to ask of her new coworkers.

They took the elevator back down to the ground floor and stopped into the cafe across from the police station. Julia loaded up two carrying trays with enough coffee to caffeinate the whole homicide department. When they got there, Renee and Ariel were sitting at their desks working through the cold case files, and they said Tate and Lena were out on a case.

"With Arlen?" Tom asked.

"No, Arlen is, uh…" Renee looked nervous, like she was trying not to tattle. At least she had one redeeming quality.

"She's doing engagement stuff, isn't she?" Tom guessed.

Ariel grinned huge. "She finally settled on a ring and she's picking it up from the jeweler! She said she'd show it to us when she got back."

"She took her lunch break to do it," Renee hurried to add. "And we didn't have a whole lot going on around here."

Tom held up a hand. "Calm down, little snitch. Nobody cares."

Julia smirked internally – maybe a little externally too – and then started passing out coffees.

"Thanks! What've you two been up to?" Ariel asked. "Out on an interesting case?"

"Same one we've been working," Julia said. She caught them up on Kyle's worsening condition, and the fact that they still had no idea what motive someone could have for poisoning him and Brandon Hawthorne.

Basically, she'd been working her first case in a new city for several weeks and she still had jack shit. It wasn't a good feeling.

"Kyle Brody has had no visitors as far as we can tell," Tom said. "so unless someone snuck into his room to give him more mushrooms, anything he consumed had to be on him when he arrived at the ER."

"Speaking of sneaky visitors..." Julia swiveled to face her computer and logged into her email. "Surveillance footage is here... all three-hundred-some hours of it. Who wants some?"

"Oh, so this is less of a nice gesture and more of a bribe," Renee said, pointing to her coffee.

"Send me some files, I'll help," Ariel said.

"Thank you, I really appreciate it," Julia said and forwarded a day's worth of footage to her.

"Me too," Renee grudgingly said.

"Send it here too," Tom growled, slumping into his seat. "The gruntwork begins."

Julia parceled out the files to everyone, and started in on her own. It really was dull, eye-glazing work to watch a full day's security footage in fast-forward. But with her new crew sharing in the workload, it wasn't so bad.

25
EMERY

*E*mery was on her way to the lab the next morning when she passed the break room and saw Monica bracing herself against the counter.

"Whoa, are you okay?"

She went in and put a hand on Monica's shoulder, preparing to catch her just in case she fainted or something. *Please don't be in labor,* her mind raced. It was too early for that and Emery had no idea what to do if it happened.

"Just trying not to puke," Monica reassured her. "Somebody thought it would be cute to microwave eggs... oh god, just saying the word is too much."

"Remind me to never get pregnant," Emery said, taking Monica's hand and leading her out of the break room, away from the devil smells that were setting her off and which Emery barely even noticed.

"My tea," Monica whined. "I came in here to make chamomile."

"I'll take care of it, how far did you get?"

"It's in the microwave," she said. "Still cold."

"Okay, go to my office, I'll bring it to you."

Monica nodded. "I keep waiting for this phase of the pregnancy to be over, but I might be one of those lucky women who get morning sickness until the day I deliver."

She left in a hurry, and Emery made the tea for her. She found her best friend sitting in her office with her eyes closed, and she set the cup of tea down in front of her. Then she went around her desk and rummaged in a drawer.

"Here." She handed a small pouch to Monica. "Candied ginger – good for nausea. It helped me when I had that stomach virus last fall and I had to come to work anyway because my petri dishes weren't going to observe themselves."

Monica opened the pouch and popped a large sugar-coated piece of ginger into her mouth. She bit into it and her eyes immediately went wide. "Oh my fucking god, what *is* this?"

"I told you, candied–"

"Candied Satan," Monica said, spitting it out in Emery's trash can and then chugging half her cup of tea. She looked reproachfully at Emery. "Why would you do that to me? I thought we were friends."

Emery couldn't help laughing. "I'm sorry, it's a polarizing food. I truly thought it would help."

"I hated it."

"Dully noted."

Monica chucked the package back across the desk,

then said, "You know what? I'm too busy being disgusted to feel nauseated, so I guess it did work."

Emery laughed again. "You're welcome."

"Thank you for the tea," Monica added. She sipped the rest and Emery sat patiently with her until Monica said, "I can still smell the egg."

"The break room is all the way down the hall."

"It's in the cup. It transferred or something."

"Microwaved tea is always a last resort anyway. I can make you something from my Keurig," Emery offered.

"No, just distract me until the nausea passes," Monica said, putting aside the cup. "How's it going with your sexy detective?"

"I really like her," Emery sighed, her shoulders slumping.

"Is that a bad thing?"

Emery chewed on her lip. "I'm not sure she wants me to get invested. So far it's been pretty physical, which, don't get me wrong, has been great. But I want it to be more."

"Why can't it be?"

"It isn't up to me," Emery said. "If it was, then I'd put myself out there, tell her I want more than just…" Even though they were alone in her office, she lowered her voice to say, "*sex.*"

"I mean, I know it takes two to tango – in every sense," Monica said, "but I'm failing to see the issue here. Why don't you tell her that, and see what she says? I'd put money on the fact that she wants to date you too, or you wouldn't have found as many excuses as you two have to see each other."

"She can't," Emery said.

"Why, is she already married?"

"No."

"Engaged?"

"No."

"Allergic?"

Emery raised an eyebrow at her, and Monica chuckled.

"Just trying to eliminate obstacles. Tell me already."

"She's in hiding."

Monica's eyes went wide. "Excuse me? From what, the mob?"

"From an abusive ex."

"Oh shit."

"Yeah, back in Michigan," Emery said.

She'd promised Julia she would never breathe a word of her previous identity, and she wasn't sure how much she could share about the situation as a whole. But she'd always talked to her best friend about everything – it was how Emery processed things. She tried to be as vague as possible, giving Monica only the broad strokes, and even the little she did divulge was a weight off her chest. She could only imagine how it felt for Julia, carrying all that around by herself.

"Julia is worried that her ex could still be looking for her, and she thinks something bad could happen to me as a result," Emery said. "I'm just worried about Julia herself, whether she's safe."

Monica nodded along. "Sure, those are both real threats. Why couldn't she press charges back home?"

"She has a restraining order, but I guess the ex never did anything bad enough to put her in jail or anything like that," Emery said. "She pushed hard enough to freak Julia out, to make her change her name and move two states away, but she never did anything Julia could prove was her."

"And she's a detective, so I'm sure she knows."

Emery chewed her lip some more. "I'm a little worried that part of it *was* the fact that she's a detective. Maybe she didn't go after the ex to the fullest extent because she didn't want people judging her, thinking she couldn't handle herself – in her personal life or on the job."

"Well, she needs to get the ex's picture plastered all over the police station just in case she dares to show up here."

"I agree."

"So... what's her real name?" Monica lowered her voice to ask, coy and curious. Conflict twisted in Emery's chest, but before she had to respond, Monica shook her head and held up a hand. "Never mind, I shouldn't have asked. The fewer people who know, the better."

Emery relaxed in her seat. "I can tell you it's beautiful and unusual and classy just like her."

Monica grinned. "You've got it bad."

"Do not."

"Do too," she smirked again, taking another sip of her tea.

"Okay fine, I do," Emery agreed. Then she stood up. "That's enough gossip. I better get back to my research while I have the time."

"Go for it." Monica started to get up, then closed her eyes. "I'm just going to sit here and finish my tea, if you don't mind."

"Sure. Feel better soon."

26
JULIA

*J*ulia's eyes were about an hour past glazed over when she became aware of a buzzing sound in her periphery.

She'd been staring at surveillance footage for the past four hours – multiple different angles and locations around the ICU covering the entire time that Kyle Brody had been there. The other detectives helped out when they could, but this wasn't their case and they were getting called out to scenes so they couldn't dedicate themselves to this.

Not that she'd ask them to – being forced to scan through this much surveillance footage was practically a violation of the Geneva Conventions.

But being a detective wasn't all glamorous car chases and thrilling discoveries. Sometimes it was a whole-ass pot of coffee and three hundred hours of CCTV.

So far she'd seen a lot of different nurses and doctors and cleaning staff coming and going from Kyle's room, but zero visitors, just as Dr. Nasir told her. She'd written down the names of everyone she recognized, and timestamps for those she didn't, and her next step would be cross-referencing the hospital's timeclock to make sure everyone who *was* there was supposed to be.

But right now, she was sure that if she sat in that seat, staring at that screen for just a single second longer, she was going to go blind.

She got up and walked the length of the department, stretching her legs and talking herself into the fact that she deserved a break. Then she took out her cell and dialed Emery's number.

"Hey, I was just thinking about you," the gorgeous scientist answered, and warmth bloomed in Julia's chest.

"You were?"

"Yeah, I missed you."

"I've missed you too," Julia smiled.

"What's up?"

Julia filled her in on the surveillance footage madness, and the fact that the evidence techs' initial exam showed no signs of spores or any other trace evidence of *A. bisporigera* on the personal effects Kyle Brogan had with him in the hospital.

"So does that mean he didn't take that second dose himself?"

"That or he did a really good job of disposing the evidence," Julia said. She glanced around the department, but everyone else had been making themselves scarce ever since she started asking them to review surveillance. Then she sat up a little taller as an idea struck her. "Hey, what are you doing tomorrow night?"

"Mmm, nothing," Emery said. "Why?"

"It's Friday night and a bunch of the county employees go to the Taphouse for drinks every week," Julia said. "I went last week and it was pretty fun."

"You're inviting me to come meet your friends?"

"My coworkers," Julia said. "I haven't been in town long enough to cross the friend barrier. But yes, I'd love it if you came."

"What time?"

Julia gave Emery all the details, and she promised to meet her there.

"I can't wait," Emery said, and Julia could hear in her voice how much she meant it.

The next day at quitting time, Julia slid away from her desk with a groan. Her eyes were red and dry from all that screentime, but the task was finished and she had the company of a beautiful woman to look forward to shortly. She practically skipped up the street to the Taphouse with her fellow detectives.

"You have a lot of pep in your step for someone who just watched three hundred hours of surveillance," Renee commented.

"Not quite three hundred – you, Ariel and Tom watched a couple days' worth," Julia said. "But I can't say

I'm not glad that's over. Not a single non-staff visitor went into that hospital room, but at least now we know."

"I happen to know there's another reason she's excited right now," Tate chimed in.

Julia raised an eyebrow. How could she know?

"I overheard you saying goodbye to your girlfriend on the phone yesterday when I was coming back from a scene," she said.

"She's not..." Julia stopped mid-sentence. She'd had a visceral reaction to the G word, but that was just her baggage speaking. How was she going to introduce Emery to everyone when they got to the bar? They were definitely more than friends.

Maybe they should have had this conversation before she asked Emery to meet everyone. It'd been a spur-of-the-moment idea.

"Not your girlfriend?" Tate pressed.

"Is she cute?" Renee asked. "Cuz if you haven't locked it down and you're planning to introduce her to basically every queer cop and forensic investigator in the city, you may want to rethink that."

Ariel and Lena laughed, and Julia surprised herself by shooting a jealous glare at Renee. "She's my girlfriend. We haven't labeled ourselves yet, but..." She narrowly avoided the possessive word choice of *she's mine,* saying instead, "Yeah, we're dating."

Renee playfully raised her hands in surrender. "Good to know."

Then she winked.

Lord, Julia wanted to smack that smugness off her face.

The Taphouse was bustling when they arrived. A lot of the tables were already full, and delicious, greasy bar food smells abounded. Dylan and Elise from the medical examiner's office had claimed their usual high-top table near the back, and as Julia slid onto her stool, she took out her phone to text Emery, letting her know where to find them.

"Drinks?" Dylan asked. She recited Tate and Renee's drink orders from last week, which was impressive enough, then apologized when she couldn't remember what Ariel and Julia liked.

"I'm a sweet tea girl," Ariel said over the sound of the bar, "thank you."

"I actually just get whatever sounds good," Julia said. "Tonight... could you get me something light, an IPA on tap?"

"You got it," Dylan said and headed over to the bar.

"Julia's gotta stay sharp so she can protect her girlfriend from the rest of us," Renee teased.

"Oh?" Elise's eyebrow rose.

She took the liberty of filling her in on Julia's invited guest, and around the time Dylan was coming back with a round of drinks, Julia noticed Emery coming through the front door. Her heart immediately climbed into her throat, and she got up to meet her halfway.

Emery immediately scooped Julia into her arms and kissed her, then second-guessed it, asking, "Is this okay?"

"This is wonderful," Julia answered. She could feel

her coworkers' eyes on her from across the bar, and she found herself putting a little extra showiness into the kiss after Renee's comment about competing over Emery.

Emery held out her hand and Julia took it. "You ready for this?"

"Sure am."

They made a quick pitstop at the bar so Julia could buy Emery a beer, then they went over to the table. After a round of introductions that did not include the word 'girlfriend' but did include several teasing comments about the mysterious, sexy mycologist Julia had been spending so much of her time with, they all settled in to drink their beers and chat.

A couple more people from the ME's office came – the pathologist, Amelia, and her fire captain partner, Simone, and Reese and Jordan from reception and the morgue, respectively. There was shop talk, and continued speculation over when, exactly, Arlen was going to pop the question to her girlfriend, Maya, now that she had the ring.

Groups broke off and side conversations began, and Julia found herself gravitating toward Emery no matter what else was going on. They ended up in a world of their own at the two bar stools at the end of the table, leaning in and talking close in order to be heard over the music and the chatter.

"The G word *may* have been used to describe you before you got here," Julia admitted.

"The G word?" Emery asked. "Gangsta?"

Julia almost spit her beer across the table.

"Girlfriend!"

"Oh that," Emery said, looking both bashful and pleased. "You used that word?"

"One of my coworkers did." Julia had just enough alcohol in her system to make her unapologetic about staring at Emery. Her dark skin was so smooth and soft, her dimples so irrepressibly cute, her mouth a perfect cupid's bow. "I wouldn't mind, though."

Emery set down her beer bottle. "Really?"

"I mean, if you're not intimidated by all my baggage..."

Emery folded her hand over Julia's, warming her and sending tingles up her arm. "Not at all. I know you're worried about getting involved, but I like you, Julia. I can't stop thinking about you."

"I *am* worried... but I can't stop thinking about you either," Julia said, turning her hand over so their palms met and interlacing their fingers.

"Let's just take it slow," Emery suggested. "If the G word comes up, I certainly won't be upset. But if you don't want a label just yet, I understand that too."

"You're wonderful," Julia said. "And I think you deserve another drink on me."

She squeezed Emery's hand, then slipped off the stool and went to the bar for a couple more beers. When she got back, Emery was chatting with Dylan about the areas in which their careers overlapped.

"I've never even been asked to test for amatoxin in a decedent before the Hawthorne case," Dylan was saying as Julia took her spot at the table again. "I did a little with mycology in grad school, though, just in case I ever needed it."

"It's pretty rare as a cause of death," Emery agreed. "Most of my work is academic."

"And yet you've consulted on two cases in the last couple weeks," Dylan pointed out. "Related, right?"

"We haven't found the link yet, but they have to be," Julia said.

"Whatever happened with the guy who was friends with the first victim and lives in the building with the second one?" Lena asked.

"Nick," Julia said. "I talked to him. He said he'd never seen Kyle Brody around the apartment complex, didn't recognize his name. I don't think he was lying."

"But he could have been," Reese piped up, switching from a conversation going on at the other end of the table to theirs. "People lie all the time."

"Are you an investigator?" Emery asked.

"Professional gossip," Dylan answered for her. "She's our receptionist."

"I just wanted to answer phones and make a steady paycheck," Reese said, "never thought I'd spend my days overhearing stuff about murders and other gory deaths."

"Turns out she loves it," Dylan's fiancée, Elise chimed in with a smirk.

"Even the dead have gossip to share," Reese said.

"That's pretty much my whole job," Julia answered. "Finding the dirt, so to speak."

"And sometimes digging in the dirt," Emery added.

The conversation turned to the skeleton-in-the-tree

case that Renee had been working. It was turning out to be just as difficult as expected to figure out the identity, although the forensic anthropologist had determined it was a male in his forties who'd died just a few decades ago.

"So you're looking at a likely homicide, not some ancient indigenous burial site," Julia said, trying to suppress her jealousy over the case.

"Looks like it, I'll be working on this for a while unless we have a breakthrough with the ID," Renee answered.

Emery bought another round of beers for everyone and the alcohol was starting to go pleasantly to Julia's head when Emery put her arm around her shoulder.

"Is this okay?" she asked softly.

Julia snuggled into her. "It's perfect."

And then her phone buzzed in her pocket. Her thigh was pressed against Emery's leg, so they both felt it, and Julia let out a groan.

"Work?" Emery asked.

"Hope not," Julia answered, digging the phone out.

There was a text waiting for her from a number that she didn't recognize. She frowned, figuring it was probably a coworker whose number she hadn't programmed in yet.

But when she unlocked her phone and read the message, ice flooded her veins.

"Oh shit."

"What?" Emery asked.

Julia felt sick, all that euphoric warmth from the

alcohol suddenly turning on her and making her gorge rise. When she didn't answer, Emery looked over her shoulder to read the message.

I knew I'd find you eventually... I'll never give up on us. Come back home, baby – Michigan's better than Ohio anyway.

27
EMERY

*E*mery watched as Julia shoved her phone into her pocket, mumbled an excuse to the group about needing to retrieve something from the office, then hustled out of the bar.

She was halfway down the block and walking fast by the time Emery caught up to her on the sidewalk.

"Hey, Julia... wait for me, okay?"

She barely responded, muttering an apology, and she was shaking. It made Emery's guts feel like they were being squeezed and twisted, and she wanted nothing more than to do the same to the monster who made Julia react like this.

"Stop for just a second, please," she pleaded, gently taking Julia's hand.

That seemed to break her out of her panic, at least enough to respond if not enough to stop. "I have to go."

"Where?"

"I don't know."

"Can I come?"

That earned her a sideways glance and a bit of consideration. There was torment in Julia's eyes, but Emery was relieved when she said yes, even if it was in a distracted, shaky way.

So Emery kept up with her as Julia speed-walked up the sidewalk toward the police parking garage, their hands linked, wondering what the hell to say or do next. She was in uncharted territory here, and terrified of scaring Julia away. She couldn't let her go through this alone, though... whatever it was.

"It was your ex, right? Who sent the text?" she finally got brave enough to ask.

"Yeah. She figured out my new number. She knows I'm in Ohio."

"Should we go tell the chief? File a report?"

"Lot of good that's done in the past," Julia said as they turned into the parking garage. "I think I need to leave."

"Okay, we'll go home," Emery agreed. "Your place or mine?"

"I need to leave the state. It was foolish of me to think I could have a normal life here."

Emery's stomach was suddenly full of rocks and she had to resist the urge to throw her arms around Julia, cling to her with all she had. "What?"

"It's not safe here, for me or for you if I'm with you," Julia said, still panicky, then suddenly bubbling over with anger. "God damn it! I don't want to start over again! I have a good thing here."

She smacked a concrete pillar as she passed it, then immediately drew her hand back and hissed with pain.

Emery took Julia's hand, cradling her stinging palm. "I have a good thing now that you're here too. Please don't go... if you run, she wins."

A selfish thing to say, she knew it even before the words left her mouth. But anything she could say right now to convince Julia not to leave her was fair game as far as she was concerned. At least the pain from slapping the pillar seemed to have redirected the anxiety that was making her whole body shake on the way here.

"If I don't run, it's only a matter of time til she shows up here," Julia said. "And she could hurt you."

Julia let Emery pull her into a hug. "I'm not worried about that – I only care about you. If you don't want to talk to the chief about this, come back to my place. We'll strategize and figure out what to do next. I won't let her get anywhere near you, I promise."

"You don't know her," Julia mumbled against Emery's shoulder.

"Yeah, well, she doesn't know me either," Emery said. "I may be a nerdy scientist, but I can be tough when I have to. If she shows up here, I'll make her wish she hadn't."

That finally got a smile from Julia, even if it was a small one. "Are you gonna beat her up?"

"Can't say it's in my nature, but I will if I have to. Can we go back to my place now?"

Julia sighed. After a moment of thought, she said, "Make it mine, just in case I need to leave after all."

Pain stabbed at Emery's chest at the idea, but she agreed. "Let's call a rideshare – we've both been drinking."

"I'm stone-cold sober after that text," Julia said. But she let Emery get them a car, and they made the short trip to her apartment. It was Emery's first time being there, and it was clear that Julia didn't spend much time there either. The apartment was bare, with only a few essentials scattered around the place.

"You really did leave Michigan in a hurry, didn't you?" Emery asked.

She wrapped Julia in her arms again in the middle of the sparse living room, and she didn't want to let her go – now or ever. A fierce drive to protect this woman rose up whenever Emery was around her, something she'd never felt before, and which was only intensified by this scumbag ex that kept popping up.

"Basically fled the minute I got a job offer from FCPD," Julia confirmed. "Left with whatever would fit in the trunk of my car."

And you're ready to do it all over again, Emery thought sadly. Probably already would have run if Emery hadn't talked her out of it.

"I know you're scared," Emery said. "I can't pretend to know what you're going through, and I know how serious the situation is. All I want is for you to be safe... but please don't leave."

Julia looked up at her. Those dark eyes stormy, tortured, glossy with pain... but damn, she was still the hottest woman Emery had ever seen, little wisps of hair coming out of her ordinarily neat ponytail and framing her pretty face. What if this was the last time Emery ever saw her? What if she had gotten freaked out and ran and Emery didn't even get to say goodbye?

She hooked both hands around the back of Julia's head and drew her into a desperate kiss.

Julia's body responded, relaxing into her, giving in to her.

The scent of her flooded Emery's senses, the feel of her body curving against her own. The slick joy of Julia's tongue gliding over Emery's as they deepened the kiss...

I love you, Emery thought.

"I need you," she said.

"Take me," Julia breathed.

And Emery did, right there on the living room floor. Within seconds, they were a tornado of hands tearing at each other's clothes, throwing them aside and clinging to each other like their lives depended on it.

And damn if it didn't really feel like that was true. Emery had never met a woman like Julia, never even been the object of someone else's desires for more than a fling, and she'd never felt her heart fill up with another person the way it did for Julia.

It might actually explode if she left.

Buck-naked, Emery dropped to her knees in front of Julia. She lifted one creamy thigh over her shoulder and dove hungrily between her legs. Julia was dripping wet, just as desperate for this as Emery, and she laced her fingers into Emery's hair, using her head to steady herself.

"Oh God," she cried into the echoey apartment the

moment Emery's tongue touched her clit. "Oh, fuck yes..."

Her fists closed on Emery's hair, tugging at her scalp, and the sensation shot straight down between her own legs. *That's right, baby, hold onto me.* She lapped and licked and slid her fingers into Julia's wetness until she could feel her thighs shaking around her. Then Emery brought her down to the carpet.

She was about to go down on her again when Julia used her grasp on Emery's hair to tug her back up to her mouth. They kissed, Julia slicked her tongue over Emery's lip, tasting herself, and then she said, "Turn around."

"Huh?"

"I want to taste you too," she said, putting her hands on Emery's hips and nudging her into the position she wanted.

Emery got the idea, her hips braced above Julia's head as she lowered her mouth back down to her sex. Julia looped her arms around Emery's thighs, holding her tight as she guided her down to meet her mouth.

And stars exploded behind Emery's eyes.

As Julia's tongue explored every inch of her, Emery lost track of what her own mouth was doing. She just braced herself above Julia, riding the waves of pleasure that washed over her with every stroke of Julia's tongue. In what felt like seconds, she was coming, her thighs shaking uncontrollably against Julia's ears and her arms threatening to give out. A flood of arousal let loose through her whole body and Julia lapped up every last drop.

When the stars faded and Emery's vision finally returned to her, Julia's swollen, wet sex on full display in front of her, she turned to peek over her shoulder.

"So, you got what you wished for."

Julia laughed. "I'm not done yet. And neither are you."

She grinned, and Emery finally regained enough self-awareness to remember what she was doing. She bowed her head, getting to work – the best kind of work.

Julia was touching her too, slowly and gently at first, letting her body come down from her first orgasm before building back up to a second. When Emery could feel Julia's muscles beginning to contract around her fingers, Julia's mouth left her folds to ask, "Think we can come together?"

Blood rushed into Emery's head at the delicious idea. "I'd love nothing more."

"Then just keep doing what you're doing," Julia said, her mouth returning to Emery's clit and applying a bit more pressure.

Bliss shot through Emery's body from head to toe. "Right now?"

"Mmmh?" Julia's words were muffled, her lips pressed to Emery's skin.

"Are you ready?" It was all Emery could do to get those three words out, bracing herself above Julia's body. It was complete sensory overload, the scent and the taste of her, the feel of Julia's tongue between her legs... sensory overload in the best possible way.

"Almost there..."

Emery plunged two fingers into Julia's core and felt her hips bucking against her.

"Yes!" Julia gasped, and then they were tipping over the edge together, a frenzied heap of sweaty, desperate bodies grinding and coming and panting together.

What seemed like one full eternity later, Emery rolled off Julia, collapsing with her head at the foot of the bed, staring up at the ceiling and breathing hard. Her whole body vibrated, and she couldn't quite decide if she wanted to go again right now, or take a week-long nap.

She just knew she never wanted to let go of this woman.

Julia's hand caressed her thigh. She lifted her head to look at her. "Good?"

"Fucking amazing," Julia said, a grin on her face.

And that made Emery smile. An hour ago, she'd been on the verge of packing up her life here in Fox City and running. Now she was naked and clinging to her.

Emery had done that, brought her back from the brink.

At least for the moment.

She crawled up to the head of the bed, scooping Julia into her arms. "You okay?"

Julia's eyes were deep, warm, with only a hint of the storminess that had been in them before. "Better now."

"Good." Emery kissed her temple. "I want you to *want* to stay here. With me. I..." *Love you.* No, far too soon to say something like that – it'd make her run all over again. "Really like you. You don't deserve to get scared off from the life you're trying to build here just because your ex is an asshole."

Julia nestled her head into the curve of Emery's neck, and satisfaction bloomed in her chest. "I like this life."

"Me too. Say you won't leave."

Julia didn't answer that plea. It just hung there in the air, and on one level, Emery understood. If Julia felt like she was in danger, she couldn't make that promise.

On a much deeper level, though, all Emery wanted was to track down this Samantha monster, jack her up against a wall and tell her never to fuck with her woman again.

28
JULIA

*J*ulia woke the next morning to the smell of coffee being brewed. Her bed was empty, but the spot where Emery slept was still warm. Julia was just climbing out from under the covers and reaching for a robe when Emery stepped into the doorway, stark naked and holding two steaming mugs.

"Coffee?"

Julia had her eyes on something else, tracing over the long, subtle curves of Emery's body, but the caffeine was welcome too. "This is about the best thing I think I've ever seen first thing in the morning."

Emery gave her a little curtsy and a cheeky grin. "Glad I could be of service."

She handed her one of the mugs and Julia took a sip, then groaned happily. "So good. You remembered how I take it."

"I make a point of remembering things that make you

smile," Emery said. Then a shadow crossed her expression. "You're not still thinking about leaving, are you?"

Julia frowned. "I don't want to leave – you, this town, my job."

"But?"

"I don't exactly feel safe right now." She could see the anguish on Emery's features so she hurried to add, "I'm not going anywhere, at least not today. Well, I'm not leaving town anyway. I really should stop by the hospital and see if Kyle Brody is feeling up to talking. If we stand any chance of closing that case, he's going to have to start telling the truth."

"Can I come?" Emery asked, then looked bashful. "I don't mean to butt in, but I don't feel particularly safe *for* you, knowing your ex is out there... it'd make me feel a whole lot better if you'd let me come with you."

A smile crept across Julia's lips. "Be my bodyguard?"

"Something like that."

"Well, you are a part of this case," Julia pointed out. "But it's your day off and it's going to be boring. Are you sure?"

"The only thing on my to-do list is dinner with Monica but that's not for hours, and besides, I'd go anywhere with you," Emery interrupted. "Just lead the way."

So they transferred their coffee to to-go mugs and headed out. They grabbed breakfast sandwiches from a drive-through on the way to the hospital, and got there a little after eight.

The first thing Julia did was stop at the nurses' station

and show her badge. "How's Kyle Brody doing this morning?"

"He's stable for the moment," the nurse said.

Well, that didn't sound too promising. "Conscious?" Julia asked.

"Yes, but not coherent. He's got cerebral edema as a result of acute liver failure," the nurse said, and when Julia gave her an obviously confused look, she amended her statement. "There's fluid putting pressure on his brain, which is making him disoriented. We're treating him with medications right now, but if it gets any worse, he'll need surgery."

"Doesn't sound good," Julia said, noticing that Emery looked pretty grim beside her. "Has his prognosis changed?"

"His liver is shutting down," the nurse said. "We're doing everything we can, but unless he gets a transplant match, the outlook isn't good."

"And he still hasn't had any visitors?" she asked. "No parents, grandparents, no one?"

"Not when I've been on shift," the nurse said.

"Can I talk to him?"

"It probably won't do much good, but you're welcome to try," the nurse said. "I'm due to go in and check his IV anyway. I'll go with you."

They found Kyle lying in his hospital bed, his skin a distinctly yellow hue, his cheeks sunken. He was hooked up to about a dozen tubes and monitors, and he looked like he was defying fate simply by still being alive.

"Jesus," Julia murmured under her breath.

"Kyle?" the nurse said. "There's someone here to speak with you."

"Mandy?" He lifted his head, his eyes looking glazed but hopeful.

"Who's Mandy?" Emery whispered beside Julia.

"Don't know," she whispered back before raising her voice to remind Kyle who she was.

They didn't get past introductions. He was too confused to grasp the fact that she was a detective, not this Mandy woman, and too distracted by what the nurse was doing with his IV to focus on Julia.

"Did you bring me a cheeseburger? I'd kill for a cheeseburger."

"He's asked for one several times," the nurse said. "We requested one from the kitchen yesterday but when it got here, he wouldn't eat it. I don't think he actually has much of an appetite."

"Did you remember to return that movie rental, Mandy?" he asked. "I don't want another damn late fee."

Emery gave Julia a bemused look. Movie rentals? What decade was it in Kyle's head? There was no point in talking to him while he was in this state.

Julia decided to throw in the towel – she wasn't getting anything out of him in this state. "You just focus on recovering, okay, Kyle? I'll come back and see you when you're feeling more yourself."

"Okay, Mandy."

His head flopped down on the pillow and Julia led the way out of the room. She took a moment to jot down the name Mandy in her investigation notebook, Emery waiting patiently beside her. The nurse passed on her way back to the counter, saying, "Told you he was out of it."

"Call me if anything changes?" Julia asked, handing her a business card.

"Will do."

Once they were alone again and heading toward the elevators, Julia let out a sigh. "Well, that was fruitless. Thanks for coming with me anyway."

"I really hope for his sake he's high on the transplant list," Emery said. "I've never seen it in person, but I've read case studies on advanced amatoxin poisoning, and he's not in a good place right now."

"I sure hope he pulls through," Julia said, pushing the button to call the elevator. "If he can't talk to me, I don't really have any leads to go on."

The elevator dinged and the doors slid open. They had to step back as a kitchen employee pushed a big aluminum cart full of breakfast trays out of the elevator.

"Excuse me," she said, meeting Julia's gaze as she passed. And then her expression did a rapid shift – recognition, fear, and then a false neutral that Julia had been trained for years to spot.

It took Julia a moment to place her. She was wearing a kitchen uniform and a hairnet, her blonde hair pulled back in a tight bun.

And then it hit her. "Are you–"

Julia didn't get any farther than those two words before the girl shoved the meal cart at her and started bolting down the hallway.

"What the hell?" Emery said.

"Amanda Drake," Julia said. "The fucking girlfriend!"

She didn't have time to explain further. She was racing down the hall after Amanda, with a vague notion that Emery was following in her footsteps.

29
EMERY

Emery didn't think – she just took off after Julia and the woman who was desperately trying to get away from her.

The girlfriend, whatever that meant.

They trailed her down the hall and around a corner, where Julia narrowly avoided landing in the lap of a patient being transported in a hospital bed. Emery snagged her hand just in time and kept her on her feet.

"No running!" the orderly pushing the bed yelled at them both.

"Police," Julia barked back, "sorry!"

She barely lost any momentum, skirting around the bed and turning toward the sound of a door closing somewhere further up the hall.

"Where'd she go?" Emery asked.

"There's a bathroom," Julia said, pointing. "Stay here, I'll check. Shout if you see her."

"Shouldn't you have backup?" That was all Emery

had time to ask before Julia was throwing the door to the women's room open and going in.

"Yes," she said over her shoulder, and then she was gone.

And Emery was abruptly alone.

The orderly and patient had moved on and the hall was dead silent. Amanda wasn't coming back through here. If Julia guessed wrong about which door she went through, she was probably long gone.

If she'd guessed right and followed some psycho into the bathroom all by herself with no one to have her back...

Emery wasn't a cop. She didn't have a weapon and she didn't know a restraint techniques from a wrestling move, but she wasn't doing anyone any good out here in the hallway.

"Freeze! Drop it!" The words were muted by the closed door, but distinctly Julia's. That was all it took to get Emery bursting through that door too, adrenaline coursing through her veins.

The restroom had multiple stalls, and Julia was standing at the open door of the last one in the row, holding up the gun she normally wore in a shoulder holster beneath her jacket.

"Stay back," she ordered Emery the moment she caught sight of her. Then she stepped inside the stall, disappearing from view.

It was the scariest minute of Emery's life. She was waiting for a struggle, a gunshot, screaming – anything could be going on in there. It took everything she had to stay put, but all going in after Julia would accomplish would be distracting her at a crucial moment.

"I said don't move!"

"Get away from me!"

"Drop the packet!"

Then the toilet flushed and Emery heard the distinctive sound of flesh colliding with tile. Her heart jumped into her throat and she listened to a scuffle going on in the bathroom stall, wondering if she should be calling 911 to get backup.

"Emery," Julia called.

"Yes." God, it had never been sweeter to hear her own name.

"I need your help."

The adrenaline propelled her forward again – well, maybe her heart had something to do with it too.

In the stall, Julia had Amanda on the floor, straddling her hips with her belly and her cheeks pressed against the tile. Emery spared a moment of revulsion for the intimate contact with a hospital bathroom floor, but it sounded like Amanda had been asking for it, even if Emery didn't know why yet.

"My handcuffs," Julia said. "Unclip them from my belt."

She was restraining the woman, hands clamped around both of Amanda's wrists and pinning her hands to the floor above her head. She couldn't cuff her without Emery's help.

She did as Julia instructed, retrieving the cuffs and snapping one of them onto Amanda's left wrist.

"Okay, step back now," Julia said, and Emery did. She turned her attention to the woman beneath her. "You going to cooperate now?"

"Do you always give people concussions for trying to flush their stash?" Amanda retorted.

Emery looked to the toilet. There was nothing in it, but she did see a baggie full of white powder lying on the floor. Julia must have tackled Amanda just before she dropped it in the bowl.

"Do *you* really think I'm going to buy that you brought recreational drugs to work?" Julia asked, then took advantage of Amanda's distraction to yank the cuffed hand behind her back. "Didn't care to mention that you work in the kitchen here when you came into the station, huh? What happened to the home delivery meal prep bullshit that you fed us?"

"It wasn't bullshit, I just got this job," Amanda grunted against the tile. "I started two weeks ago."

"And I wonder why," Julia said. She grabbed Amanda's other wrist and the woman finally stopped fighting, allowing her to draw the hand behind her back and snap it into the handcuffs without the pain this time. "Kyle killed Brandon so you were going to kill him the same way, is that it?"

"If he dies, he'll deserve it," Amanda said.

Julia secured her gun now that the suspect was restrained, then got to her feet. "Sit against that wall if you want, or keep lying on the bathroom floor – I don't care. But don't move a muscle toward that door until I tell you to."

A little inappropriate shiver of desire worked its way through Emery at listening to her girlfriend lay down the law.

Amanda sat up awkwardly, then tried to position her back to the wall nearest the baggie of white powder. Julia caught on immediately.

"Uh-uh, that wall," she said, pointing to the other corner of the stall. Then she turned to Emery, pointing at the baggie. "Would that still do the job? Mushrooms in a powdered form, sprinkled over food maybe?"

"Yeah, sure would."

Julia nodded. "I've gotta call backup and get an evidence tech down here to collect that. Gotta test the whole cabinet full of food from the kitchen just to be safe." She turned to Amanda to say, "And then we're gonna go downtown and have a good, long talk." She turned back to Emery. "It's going to be a long day – I'm sorry I–"

"It's your job," Emery interrupted. "It's fine."

"Well, if you want to go..."

"If you want me to stay – if I'm allowed to stay – I'd love to watch you work." *And use all these images of you being a bossy, take-charge detective later on in the bedroom,* she thought.

"You can stay," Julia said, then added a quick wink. "I want you to stay."

"Get a room," Amanda snarled from the floor.

"Get a good lawyer," Julia shot right back at her. "You'll need one."

It only took a couple minutes for backup to arrive –

the uniformed officer stationed outside Kyle Brogan's room came as soon as dispatch sent out the call. It took longer to do everything they needed at the scene before Julia could take Amanda to the police station. The evidence techs were still taking samples from the food cabinet when it was time to go. Julia hauled Amanda up to her feet and walked her out of the hospital, uniformed cops on either side of her just in case she got any more bright ideas about trying to run again.

There was a squad car waiting on the sidewalk when they got outside, its light bar flashing.

"Meet you downtown," Julia told Amanda.

"Can't wait," Amanda gritted back at her.

Emery stood beside Julia, watching the two uniformed cops load the cuffed woman into the back seat of their car, then they watched it pull away from the curb.

"Last chance," Julia told Emery. "You sure you don't want me to drop you off at your place before I go in? Interrogations can take a long time."

"She got caught red-handed."

"Doesn't matter, she'll probably play innocent like she did last time Tom and I talked to her."

"There's nowhere I'd rather be than with you," Emery said. "Besides, I can always get a rideshare if I end up bored to tears."

As they walked toward the parking deck where Julia's car waited, Emery slipped her hand into Julia's. "Anybody ever tell you how sexy you are when you're apprehending criminals?"

Julia shot her a sidelong smirk. "Nope. Is somebody about to start now?"

"Hell yes," Emery answered. "You're an impressive woman, Julia Taylor. I'm so proud to call you mine."

When they got to the precinct, they went straight up to the interrogation rooms on the same floor as the homicide department. Well, there may have been a bit of making out in the elevator, prompted by all the adrenaline. But they went pretty much straight there.

Tom was waiting in the hall, having been looped in by the two officers who brought Amanda to the station.

"You want back in on this?" Julia asked when she saw him.

"Oh yeah," Tom replied. "This the mycologist?"

Emery was pleased to see Julia's cheeks color slightly at that, and even more pleased with her answer.

"Yes, but she's not here purely in a professional capacity," she said.

Before she got anything else out, Tom broke into a wide grin. "You two are an item?" He clapped his hands together, then held one up for a high five. "The great PD matchmaker strikes again!"

"You did not matchmake us," Julia objected, refusing his high five. Emery took it just because it was rude to leave someone hanging.

"Who brought you out on that hospital death call?

Who gave you the number for the mycology department at Fox U?" Tom challenged. "That started the ball rolling, and here you are now."

Julia rolled her eyes. "Fine, whatever. Emery's just going to observe, but it'll be nice to have her here in case we have any technical questions about what Amanda has to say."

"I'll be surprised if she says anything," Tom answered, switching just like that into work mode. "I heard you were pretty tough on her at the hospital."

"She threw a meal cabinet at me and tried to slam a bathroom stall door in my face," Julia said. "Excuse me if we're not besties at the moment."

She showed Emery into a room right next to the one Amanda was being held in. It had a two-way mirror that took up most of one wall, through which she could see Amanda sitting at a stainless-steel table, hands cuffed to a ring welded to its center. She was sitting almost creepily still, and staring into a corner.

"What's she looking at?" Emery asked.

"Security camera," Tom said, nodding to a table full of recording equipment on the wall behind Emery. Sure enough, there was a video monitor there, and Amanda was staring straight into it, an eerily dead look in her eyes.

"Yeah, I think I'll just stick to the mirror," Emery said, shuddering.

"If you hear anything that doesn't sound right regarding the toxin, anything you want us to dig deeper on, push this button," Julia said, pointing to one hard-wired into the wall by the window. "It's an intercom, but don't ask your question over it – just ask Detective Logan or me to step out for a moment and we'll know what you mean."

"Monica's going to be jealous I got to actually be part of the interrogation," Emery smirked. "She watches *so* much *CSI*."

"This is a bit different from TV," Tom said, "but I bet you'll have some brag-worthy details to share nonetheless."

With that, he left the room and Julia took a quick step closer to Emery. "You good in here?"

"Yep, don't worry about me – go do your job," she reassured her.

Julia kissed her, briefly but passionately, and then she disappeared out the door too. Emery turned back to the window, where Amanda was still staring blankly at the camera mounted high in the corner of the room.

30

JULIA

"Probably goes without saying, but I'm taking 'good cop,'" Tom said just before they entered the interrogation room. "And in the future, work on not being so antagonistic toward suspects right off the bat."

"I know," Julia said, hating to be chastised for something she learned in her first week of detective school. "I couldn't help it with this one – Brandon Hawthorne was her *boyfriend* and she had to have known who killed him, but she had the nerve to sit in the very room she's in now and lie to us so she could take her own revenge."

"You think a murderer is going to be honest and fair?" Tom asked, then pushed the door open. Just like that, his demeanor switched once again and he was the quintessential good cop. "Amanda, hi, sorry to keep you waiting. You need anything, a bottle of water?"

"You could take these cuffs off," she said, then

gestured as best she could to Julia. "I think she was trying to cut off my circulation when she put 'em on."

"I was trying to restrain you," Julia said. "You were resisting."

"I was on my belly on a bathroom floor," Amanda shot back.

"Because you ran," Julia said without missing a beat. The good cop technique worked so much better for getting confessions, but damn if it wasn't nice to tell a suspect exactly what she was thinking for once.

She perched on the edge of the table, close enough to keep Amanda from getting too comfortable, and Tom came around the other side to remove the handcuffs. When he was done, Amanda cradled her wrists to her chest, rubbing them like she'd just narrowly avoided losing her hands. Drama queen.

"Better?" Tom asked.

"Yes," Amanda said, catching on to who was more her friend in this room. "Thank you."

He took the chair across the table from her, and Julia went silently to the third chair in the room, pushed up against the wall near the door. She didn't sit, she just wanted to give her a little bit of breathing room so she'd open up.

When Amanda finally stopped nursing her poor, sensitive wrists, Tom asked, "Why don't you tell me what happened at the hospital this morning?"

He got an extremely rose-colored version of events, in which Amanda was just innocently going about the duties of her job when a cop with a preconceived notion of her came out of nowhere and chased her into the restroom. Julia clenched her jaw, resisting the urge to defend herself even though she already knew Tom wasn't buying this.

"And you told Detective Taylor that the job is a new one," Tom said. "If I recall, the last time we spoke to you, you were a prep cook."

"That's right," Amanda said. "I wanted something a little less demanding, something that didn't require me to work evening shifts."

"And if we call your old boss at your last job, what will he have to say about your leaving?" Tom pressed.

"He'll probably be pissed that I didn't give him notice," Amanda said, "but I was always a good worker for him. He likes me."

"And why didn't you give notice?"

"When a good opportunity comes up, you gotta take it."

"How'd you hear about the hospital job?" Tom asked.

"Personal connections," she answered. "A friend of a friend works there too." She shot an angry look at Julia. "Well, I guess I should start saying I *worked* there, past tense, because who would want to keep somebody who got cuffed and hauled away by the cops while they were on the job?"

"If you get fired, I think it'll have more to do with your poisoning patients," Julia retorted, "or maybe the fact that you'll be missing shifts due to being in prison."

"I didn't poison anyone," Amanda said, going on the defensive just like Julia wanted.

"So you're telling me the white powder in that baggie you were trying to flush is something other than destroying angel mushrooms?" she shot back. "Amanda, it would be a smart move to just tell us the truth now, maybe earn yourself some goodwill down the line, instead of denying it all the way up until we get the lab results back."

"If you did have something to do with Brandon and Kyle's exposures, it would look good that you were forthcoming with us," Tom added. "You know, demonstrate some remorse by being honest now."

That was when Amanda's eyes went scarily cold. "What if I don't have any remorse?"

"Just tell us what happened, Amanda," Tom prompted.

It looked like she was on the verge of spilling it all, but in Julia's experience, it was rarely so easy. And it wouldn't be in Amanda's case, either. Instead of a confession, what they got was hysterics.

Suddenly Amanda was bawling, and through her tears, Julia could make out small snippets of her sobbed words. "I would never hurt Brandon! I loved him! It's all his fault!"

"Brandon's fault?" Tom asked.

"Kyle!" Amanda gasped, like she was struggling to breathe through her tears. "He killed Brandon! He poisoned him."

"Why would he do that?" Tom asked. "We couldn't find any evidence that they even knew each other."

And who is Kyle to Amanda? Julia wondered from

her place in the corner, but it wasn't the time for the bad cop to chime in.

"They didn't," Amanda continued to blubber through her words.

"Why would Kyle poison someone he didn't know?" Tom pressed.

"Awfully convenient that he's too sick to defend himself against this accusation," Julia couldn't help adding. Amanda shot her a glare.

"That piece of shit deserved everything he got and more," she said, the coldness back in her eyes even as she continued to cry.

"Why?" Julia asked.

"Because he hurt me!"

Julia and Tom both knew enough to stay silent, let the moment expand as long as it had to. Amanda cried, head in her hands. After what felt like one and a half eternities, she pulled herself together and lifted her head. Tears stained her cheeks and snot ran down her upper lip, but she didn't seem to notice.

"He was my ex," she said, "from high school."

"Kyle was?" Tom clarified.

Amanda nodded. "He was abusive. It took me years to get up the nerve to leave him – I don't know why. I finally did it last year and I thought it was over at that point. I never knew what he was capable of until I started dating Brandon."

Tom reached for a box of tissues resting on the window frame of the two-way mirror. He offered Amanda one and she accepted it.

While she wiped the snot away, he asked, "What happened, Amanda?"

"We ran into him," she said.

"Kyle?"

She nodded. "I didn't know he lived in that building. Me and Brandon were picking up his friend, Nick. We were gonna go for a hike, but Kyle was in coming out as we were going in and he spotted me holding Brandon's hand. He lost his shit. Started ranting and raving about how I *belonged* to him. I never went back to the apartment complex again, but I guess it was enough. He started stalking us after that."

"How long ago was that?"

Amanda thought for a moment. "Maybe two months?"

"Did he ever confront the two of you again?"

"No, he'd just do little things to make sure we knew he was around," she said. "Write things on Brandon's car window, ring my doorbell in the middle of the night when he knew Brandon was there. That kind of stuff."

Julia's stomach went sour as her mind went immediately to Sam, and everything clicked into place. Everything Amanda had done, lying low, switching from Mandy to Amanda, lying about her connection to Kyle… it made sense because it was what Julia would have done. She *had* done a lot of it to get away from Samantha.

I know where you are, the text taunted her. Would it stop with a text like she'd been trying to tell herself, or not until one of them was dead?

And what if Samantha set her sights on Emery?

The thought made her want to be sick on the spot. She couldn't fool herself anymore, couldn't tell herself she was overreacting when she saw the worst-case scenario right here in front of her. She knew how stalker cases could play out.

Bloody and violent.

Awful.

She swallowed hard and listened as Tom asked questions about restraining orders and police reports.

"Kyle started off in a bad place," Amanda explained. "His parents died in a car accident when he was really young and he was raised by an aunt and uncle that were less than perfect role models. He never had much drive to do anything with his life, even when I was with him, trying to get him to go to college or get some vocational training. But when I broke up with him, it seemed to be the motivation he needed. He told me he was going to apply to colleges."

"Did you keep in contact with him?"

"No, I didn't want anything to do with him – I just didn't want to do anything to derail him when he was finally getting his life together," Amanda said. "I thought Brandon and I could just... wait him out. I thought he'd get tired of harassing us and leave us be."

"Stalkers rarely operate like that," Tom said, shaking his head sadly.

"I know that now," Amanda said, the tears beginning to flow again. "He killed my boyfriend!"

Julia's stomach flip-flopped again. She was playing the same dangerous game as Amanda right now.

"I need to step out a moment," she said.

Tom looked to the two-way mirror, confused because there hadn't been any signal that Emery wanted to talk to them. "Fine, grab Ms. Drake a bottle of water while you're out there."

"Sure," Julia said. She walked as calmly as she could out of the room, took five steps down the hall and entered the viewing room, and the moment Emery's eyes met hers, she burst into tears.

"Whoa, babe, what's wrong?"

"Were you listening?"

"Yeah."

"I don't want that to be us!"

Emery was at her side in an instant, wrapping her arms around Julia in a fierce hug. "It won't be."

"It will if I don't do something about Sam," she said. "We have to stop her or she's going to show up here and..."

Hurt you. Kill you. She couldn't even say the words.

Emery read the silence anyway, and held her tighter. "No, she won't. We'll make sure every cop in this county has her picture."

"It's not enough," Julia shook her head.

"What do you want to do?"

"I... I don't know."

Emery lifted Julia's chin, using her thumbs to brush her cheeks dry. Their eyes were locked on each other, their bodies pressed together, and all Julia wanted to do was protect Emery – from her own dark past, from anything and anyone who might want to hurt her now, from every bad thing that could ever happen to her.

"I love you."

The words came out before she realized they'd been on the tip of her tongue.

She was about to apologize because they'd only known each other a couple of weeks, but Emery said, "I love you too," and mashed her mouth against Julia's.

The kiss was deep, penetrating all the way to Julia's belly and turning that sour feeling into a much sweeter sensation of butterflies and hope. Her story didn't have to end like Amanda's. She could do better.

She *would* do better.

"I need to get back in there," she apologized. "I just had to tell you how I felt."

"I'm glad you did."

Emery kissed her again, then squeezed her hand and let her go. Julia asked Emery if she looked okay after the crying ("You look perfect."), grabbed a bottled water out of the break room up the hall, and then headed back into the interrogation room.

She found that Tom had moved his chair around the side of the table, leaning in toward Amanda in a comforting posture, really playing up the good cop angle. Apparently it was working, because Amanda was sobbing and spilling the beans.

"I just didn't see any other way out," she was saying.

Julia set the water bottle on the table as inconspicuously as possible then went to sit by the door, trying not to be noticed so Amanda would keep talking.

"I didn't want to kill him... not at first. I just... I had to pay him back for what he did to Brandon!"

"How did you know he was the one who gave Brandon the mushrooms?" Tom asked gently.

"We used to go out foraging with my uncle back in high school," she said, "He taught us about destroying angels so we'd never eat them on accident. Kyle wanted me to know exactly who killed Bradon, and I did, the minute I heard how he died."

"So you chose the same mushrooms to pay Kyle back," Tom said.

"He was never gonna leave me alone!" Amanda wailed. "I did everything short of leaving town, and I couldn't do that cuz my whole family is here. My life is here."

"Brandon was here," Tom added.

"Yes! And everything was going fine until we ran into Kyle in the apartment complex," she said. "If that never happened, Brandon would still be here."

Tom nudged the bottled water closer to her, and she took the cue to have a drink, take a breather. They all sat in silence for a moment, then Tom asked, his voice soft, "How did you do it?"

Amanda pressed her lips together so tightly the color drained out of them. Julia wondered if she was going to answer, or clam up and refuse to speak. But then she did, a hardness taking over her voice.

"I baked him a casserole," she said. "I brought it over to his apartment. I told him that his plan with Brandon worked, that now that he was gone..." Her voice cracked, but she quickly regained control. "I told him I missed him and I wanted him back."

"And he believed it?" Julia asked, trying to imagine the desperation required to eat a mushroom dish with a woman whose life you just got done destroying with the very same mushrooms.

"I made it believable," Amanda shrugged. "Plus, I sat there with him while he ate. I made sure he cleaned his plate. I took some for myself too, but he was so busy congratulating himself on winning me back, he never noticed that I didn't eat a bite."

"And it put him in the hospital, but he knew what to look for so he got there fast enough," Tom said. "He started to recover. And that's when you took the hospital kitchen job as an excuse to get near him again?"

Amanda just nodded.

"But why did you dose him a second time?" Julia prompted. "Why not let the first one be the warning you wanted to give him and let it go?"

"He killed my boyfriend!" she cried, worked up all over again. "He believed me so readily when I said I wanted him back. The more I thought about it, the more sure I was that I'd never be rid of him unless he was dead."

"Or in prison," Tom suggested. "You could have told us what he did to Brandon. You knew when we interviewed you before, didn't you?"

"Yes," she said, resigned. "I thought about it, I really did. But I decided I had to kill him myself. It was the only way to be *sure* he was never going to be able to hurt me again."

Tom passed her the tissues, she swiped at the snot collecting on her upper lip, and then she looked up at him.

"But the bastard just keeps on surviving!"

"You still want him to die, after all this?" Julia asked. "Even sitting here in the police station, knowing you'll be charged with murder if he dies?"

Attempted murder, even if he pulls through, she thought. That was up to forty years in prison. Amanda could be of retirement age by the time she got out, all because she chose a bad guy when she was a teenager and couldn't get rid of him.

But the cold expression in Amanda's eyes remained. "I do want him to die. He deserves it for what he did to Brandon, and to me."

31
EMERY

Julia stepped out of the interrogation room about fifteen minutes after she and Tom got Amanda's confession. Amanda was still working on a written version of her statement, but Tom told Julia he could take it from there.

She met Emery in the observation room. "So, I guess that's your first Fox County case in the books," Emery said. "Good work."

"It's not over quite yet," Julia said. "We can't just take her word that Kyle is the one responsible for Brandon's death. Best case scenario, he recovers enough to talk and decides to tell the truth when we confront him."

"And if not?"

"We'll just have to double down on our search for physical evidence," she said. "A deeper inspection of Kyle's apartment, to start off with. Try to either confirm or deny Amanda's story."

"Do you think it's true?" Emery asked.

Julia sighed. "Probably. I hate to rely on personal experience when it comes to a case, but it all rings true from what I know of being with Samantha. I didn't detect any deception when Amanda was talking about her relationship with Kyle. And speaking of Sam... you up for being an emotional support human?"

"You ready to talk to the chief?"

"No better time than the present," Julia said with a resigned sigh.

They walked through the homicide department hand-in-hand and Emery hung back for a moment while Julia knocked on the chief's door.

"Come in," he called, and Julia motioned for Emery to follow.

Inside, a slightly portly man who looked to be in his fifties sat behind a cluttered desk. A blonde in a police uniform sat across from him, and they both had take-out sandwiches laid out in front of them.

"Sorry to interrupt," Julia said. "I can come back."

"We're just having lunch," the chief said. "This is my daughter, Court."

"We've met around the building," Julia said. "Didn't know you were the chief's daughter, though I probably should have guessed – same last name, right?"

"Wilson, yeah," Court said, then shot her dad a disapproving look. "Though I keep asking him not to tell people that."

"What is it, a secret?" he shot back. Then he turned back to Julia, setting his sandwich down. "You're one of my new hires in homicide, right?" Julia nodded. "What can I do for you?"

"Well, first off, this is Emery Ellison," Julia said, gesturing for her to step into the room. Emery came to her side. "She's a mycologist over at the university and she's been consulting for us. She's also..." Julia looked at Emery and smiled. "My partner."

"You don't need to fill out a relationship disclosure form if she's just consulting," the chief said.

Julia laughed nervously. "No, actually, I just wanted her here for emotional support, if that's okay."

The chief's expression turned serious and he looked at his daughter. "Honey, can I take a rain check on this lunch date? Sounds like duty calls."

"Sorry," Julia apologized, but Court waved her away.

"It's no problem, I eat with him all the time," she said. "Only way to make sure he doesn't have a burger and a milkshake for lunch every day."

She packed up her own lunch and left, pulling the door closed behind her. Then the chief gestured to the two empty chairs across from his desk. "Have a seat and tell me what's going on."

They sat, and Emery held Julia's hand while she told the chief all about her ex – including the rock through her apartment window back in Grand Rapids and the creepy text she received at the bar just the other day.

"I don't mean to bring my drama to work with me, but she's tried to use my job to manipulate me in the past," she said. "I don't want it to happen again here."

"It's not drama, stalking is serious criminal behavior,"

the chief said, and Emery instantly liked him for taking her girlfriend's safety seriously. "However, if you have a restraining order in place, I'm not sure there's much more we can do other than circulate her photo, make sure everyone in the station knows to look out for her. Have you already told your department?"

Julia shifted in her seat. "I don't want to get off on the wrong foot with them, make them think I can't handle myself."

"I doubt they would think that," the chief said. "And I don't have to tell a veteran officer like you that keeping secrets from your team isn't a good idea."

She frowned, and Emery tightened her hold on Julia's hand. "No, I know that. I was just hoping there was something we could do to end this, once and for all."

The chief sat back in his chair. "What did you have in mind?"

Julia let out a huff, and Emery wondered if she was thinking about Amanda Drake, about the lengths she went to so she could feel safe from her own stalker ex. Lengths Emery hoped Julia would never feel compelled to go to.

"I don't know," Julia put her hand to the bridge of her nose, like she was trying to stave off a headache. "I just don't think I can take another six months of living like I did in Michigan, constantly looking over my shoulder, waiting for her to show up outside my house, *inside* my workplace, in parking lots..."

"Could we lure her in?" Emery asked. "Catch her in the act, if she's going to be making threats anyway?"

The chief's hands went up instantly. "The police can't be involved in anything like that. It's entrapment, just as illegal as stalking."

Ah yes, if Emery had run that idea past Monica, she surely would have used her *CSI* knowledge to tell her so. It had just come to her in the spur of the moment, born out of desperation.

"Isn't there anything we can do?" Emery asked. "This woman is making Julia's life hell."

"We can put a security detail on you," Chief Wilson told Julia. "We can make sure you're safe, circulate that photo, and if she *does* show up here, we'll nail her feet to the floor."

Julia gave another one of those resigned sighs, this one heartbreaking in its tenor. "You're right... that's all there is to do. Can you put a detail on Emery too?"

"I don't know if I want that," Emery tried to object.

"I'm not gonna let you wind up like Brandon Hawthorne," Julia said, her tone leaving no room for argument.

The chief sat forward in his chair again. "Look, I know you don't *want* to see this woman again, but you know how stalker cases work – they escalate. If she's sending you threatening text messages and saying she knows where you live, it's likely she's planning to violate the restraining order. We can put her away *without* the entrapment when she does decide to act." He looked to Emery, then back at Julia. "And yes, I will assign an officer to your partner as well because I can see the risk."

Julia stood and put her hand out across the desk.

"Thank you, Chief. I'm sorry to bring this problem into the precinct."

He stood too, shaking her hand. "It's my job to make sure the citizens of this city are safe, and that includes my employees. There's nothing to apologize for. Besides, what I hear from Tom is you're an asset to the department."

Julia and Emery left the chief to his lunch, and went into the hall. Once the chief's door was closed and they were alone, Emery pulled Julia into a hug. "How'd you feel about that?"

"Not as good as I would have if the chief had said, 'let's haul her ass in right now and throw her in jail,'" she smirked. "He said Tom is speaking highly of me. So weird, I thought he hated me."

"So now what do we do?"

"With our lives?"

"With the afternoon," Emery laughed. "Do you have more work to do to close the amatoxin case?"

"I still have to go talk to Kyle Brogan again, get his side of the story," she said. "But I doubt a couple hours have improved his condition any. Right now all I can do is wait and see if he pulls through." She smiled up at Emery. "And we can wait at my place if you want. I'm exhausted, and I want to thank you for being my bodyguard today."

She winked, then turned toward the stairwell.

Emery wasted no time chasing after her.

"I'm so glad you're staying," Emery said the moment they were alone in Julia's apartment again. "I don't know what I would have done if you decided to leave here."

"I would have hated to leave you."

"I just might have had to follow you," Emery said. "I mean, if you wanted me to. I never want to make you feel like Sam did."

Julia pressed her lips to Emery's. "Never say that name again. I don't want it to have to cross your lips."

"I love you."

It was only the second time she'd said it, but it felt so right, the words just slipped out again. And when Julia said them back, Emery's entire body flooded with joy.

"I love you too, Emery Ellison," she said, "so damn much."

"Come here," Emery growled, pulling her closer and kissing her again. She wanted to show Julia just how much she loved her in a way that words could not.

She felt a spark, a warmth that spread from her lips all the way down to her toes. She closed her eyes and savored the way that Julia melted into the kiss. Julia nipped lightly at Emery's lower lip, eliciting a moan. Emery brought her hands up to Julia's face, her fingers lightly tracing the curves of her jaw.

Julia pulled away and looked deeply into Emery's eyes. "I'm yours... all yours," she said, her voice thick with emotion.

Emery's heart felt like it was going to burst. She

gently caressed Julia's cheek, her fingertips lingering on her soft skin. She looked back into Julia's eyes, and saw a fire there burning hotter than she'd ever seen before.

She moved her lips back to Julia's. This time, the kiss was slow and passionate, their tongues intertwining and exploring each other's mouths. Emery felt a surge of need course through her body.

Julia broke the kiss and looked into Emery's eyes. She whispered, "Let's take this to the bedroom."

Emery grinned. "Race you."

Then she took off in the now-familiar direction of Julia's bedroom. Once inside, the two of them fell into bed together, ripping each other's clothes off, hungry with need. Desire built in Emery, becoming more and more urgent with each passing moment, her skin tingling with anticipation.

When they were both fully naked, they lay down beside each other. Julia's hands began to wander over Emery's body, exploring every inch of her. A wave of pleasure coursed through her as Julia's lips lightly brushed against her neck. She closed her eyes and gave herself over to the sensation.

Julia's hands continued to move over Emery's body, her touch both gentle and demanding, her lips trailing soft kisses along the way.

Emery was relishing this slow love-making, but at the same time, she craved Julia fiercely. She pulled her closer and kissed her hungrily, ready for her.

Julia picked up the cue, her hands moving lower, touching Emery in a way that left her trembling. She felt

Julia's fingertips lightly brush against her inner thighs, then she spread Emery's legs and began to stroke her folds and the hard nub of her clit.

Emery gasped, the pleasure almost too much, the sensations overwhelming her. Her own fingers walked down over Julia's hip, circled around and plunged between her thighs, sliding into her wetness. They clung to each other, like this was the only moment, the only thing that existed in the world.

The two of them.

This pleasure.

Their bodies pressed against each other.

At last, they spilled over the edge of desire together, holding each other tight as they came, their bodies trembling against each other.

When the pleasure faded, they lay in each other's arms. Emery looked into Julia's eyes and whispered, "I love you."

Julia smiled back and whispered, "I love you too." Then she chuckled. "And I think we're gonna have to get cleaned up before you have dinner with Monica."

"Come with me," Emery said.

"Really?"

"Of course," Emery answered. "I met your friends. I'd be delighted to introduce you to my best friend."

$\mathcal{A}$n hour later, freshly showered and in clean clothes – Emery wearing something from Julia's closet that made her feel proud and naughty and loved all at the same time – they showed up at a little Italian restaurant near the lake that was Monica's favorite.

The chief had worked fast in getting them a security detail, and as they walked from the parking lot to the restaurant, Julia pointed out a man sitting behind the wheel of a black sedan, parked on the street.

"Sorry, babe, you've been replaced as my bodyguard."

"We're really going to have undercover cops following us around now, for as long as it takes S– your ex to make a move?"

Julia nodded. "You'll barely notice them – or so I hear from people I've put under protection in the past."

Emery did her best to ignore the man in the unmarked sedan. She told Julia about how Monica had discovered this restaurant in her first week at the university, and how it had turned into their go-to spot if they decided to venture off-campus for lunch. "I hope it can be your spot too now. Oh, there she is."

She pointed to where Monica stood on the sidewalk outside the restaurant, one hand smoothed over her belly. Emery felt Julia's hand clutch hers harder.

With an eyebrow raised, she asked, "Are you nervous?"

"Meeting the best friend? Yeah, a little."

"I love you, so Monica will love you," Emery said. It was already starting to feel normal to say that, and she loved it. She knew she'd never grow tired of those three words.

Monica raised her free hand. "Hey, you two. This must be the famous Julia."

"Famous?" Julia asked when they met her on the sidewalk.

Monica laughed. "You have no idea how much this one likes you. She won't stop talking about you."

"Oh, I have an idea," Julia answered with a grin.

They finished with introductions, then went inside and got a table. When the server came over, Monica ordered a lasagna dish that she talked Julia into getting as well.

"As long as it doesn't have mushrooms," she said.

Emery laughed. "Feeling squeamish?"

"For now. I'll eat them again once this case isn't so fresh in my mind."

Emery stuck with the spaghetti and meatballs she pretty much always ordered there, and they shared a basket of bread while they waited for the main course.

"So, you two," Monica said, her mouth full of bread, "tell me how things are going. Julia, I'm shocked you were able to draw this one out of her shell."

"Oh yeah?" Julia asked, intrigued.

"She's been... let's just call her a lone wolf," Monica said. "I've never known her to date anyone seriously."

"I've never met anyone worth putting myself out there for," Emery added.

"Just waiting for the right woman," Monica confirmed, "who seems to have come along at last."

Julia beamed, then stuffed a piece of bread self-consciously into her cheek. "Emery tells me you're expecting your first baby," she redirected the conversation.

They talked until the food arrived, and all through the meal there wasn't a single awkward silence. It felt immediately like all three of them had been friends for ages, and it was with a great sense of peace and rightness in the world that Emery sat back in her chair at the end of the meal. Her girlfriend and her best friend had hit it off.

They split the check two ways, Julia insisting on paying for Emery's meal for sticking by her all day. Then Monica stood up, reaching for her jacket. "Well, I better get going. The more pregnant I get, the worse I am at staying awake past nine o'clock. But I'm glad I got to meet you, Julia."

She stood up to give Monica a hug. "It was so good to meet you, too."

Monica pulled back, her face serious. "You're good for her, you know. I'm glad Emery found you."

With that, she turned to leave, and Julia looked at Emery. "That went well."

"It did," Emery agreed. "And she's right. You're better than good for me... you're perfect."

32

JULIA

Against all odds, Kyle Brogan made it back into a regular hospital room, and without an organ transplant. He had far fewer IVs and monitoring equipment attached to him. He even looked more pink than yellow in the face, although his expression turned from boredom to annoyance the moment Julia stepped into the room.

"How you feeling today, Kyle?" she asked.

"Better," he said. "Feel like I could actually leave here soon, with all my original organs too."

"You got lucky," she said, planting her feet uncomfortably close to his bedside so that she was hovering over him. "Unfortunately, it looks like your luck has run out."

"What's that supposed to mean?"

"I figured out who Mandy is," she said. "And she told us everything."

Fear shot through Kyle's eyes, quickly masked as he looked away from her. "I don't know what that means."

"No? You don't remember saying her name last time I was here?"

"I don't even remember the last time you were here."

"And I guess you didn't date Amanda Drake in high school, either. Haven't been harassing her for the last six months since she dumped you?"

"I don't feel well, I need a nurse," he complained, reaching for the call button at his bedside. Julia knocked it out of the way, not buying the act.

"What you need to do is tell me the truth, Kyle," she said. She Mirandized him and used her phone to record their conversation, setting it on the tray table beside his bed. Ordinarily an interrogation would take place at the station, but being in the hospital wasn't going to excuse Brogan from a murder charge. "We already know what happened. Amanda told us everything. So now it's time for you to give me your side of the story. Show a little remorse and a jury may go easier on you. Keep lying, though..."

She let the rest of the sentence hang there, allowing Kyle to fill in the blanks on his own.

When he turned back to her, his tone was pleading. "She poisoned me. Bet she didn't tell you that – little miss perfect with her new boyfriend and her new life that was so much better than being with me... she's the one that baked that casserole, and she tricked me into eating it."

Julia just let him talk, at long last, and he kept going.

"I bet she made me out to be some big monster," he said. "I never hit her, I never mistreated her. All I wanted was for her to love me and instead she dumped me for that prick."

"Brandon Hawthorne," Julia said.

"Holier-than-thou jock asshole," Kyle said. "Guy thought he was better than everybody else – and he convinced her that he was better than me."

"So you killed him and she turned around and tried to kill you, is that your story?"

"I wasn't *trying* to kill him," he said. "I was just..."

"Trying to send a message?" Julia arched an eyebrow. Whether it hit home that his image of himself as the nice guy in this situation was bullshit, she couldn't be sure. But he latched onto her wording.

"Exactly," he said. "Her Uncle Rick's big into mushroom hunting, started his own business doing it back when we were in high school and he used to take us out foraging with him. Never paid us for our labor, he was a dick too, but for me it was an excuse to spend time with Amanda. I figured when her new boyfriend got sick off mushrooms, she'd know exactly what that meant."

Julia narrowed her eyes. "Uncle Rick? Beasley?"

"Yeah, I think that's his last name, why?"

Julia just shook her head. "Small world. So what exactly did Uncle Rick tell you about destroying angels?"

She was trying to figure out if he knew how deadly they were, and she thought he'd try to deny it. But after several weeks at the edge of death, Kyle must have run out of energy for denials.

"He said they were toxic, some of the deadliest mushrooms out there. But Amanda knows all about them too. I thought she'd know what was wrong with her boyfriend and get his ass to the hospital."

"How did you feed them to him?"

"I waited til he ordered take-out," Kyle said. "Then I stood in the lobby of his building and pretended it was mine, took it from the delivery guy. My luck, it ended up being a pizza with mushrooms already on it. So I just added some more. I really didn't mean to kill the guy. I'm not a murderer."

Julia just shook her head pitifully at him. "You are, Kyle."

"Oh Christ," he said, reaching for the call button again. "I need drugs or something, I think I'm gonna be sick."

This time, it wasn't from the mushrooms. Julia waited for him to calm down and called in the uniformed officer who'd been waiting in the hallway. Kyle was handcuffed to his bed, where he'd stay until Dr. Nasir said he was well enough to be discharged into the custody of the police.

When Julia had finished with him and turned to go, he asked, "What about Amanda? Her boyfriend dying was an accident, but she really did try to kill me! What's gonna happen to her?"

Julia turned around in the doorway. "Amanda is not your concern, and never will be again, Kyle. Don't forget that."

33
EMERY

*E*mery's heart was pounding for a multitude of reasons.

She was walking down the sidewalk with Julia on their way to the diner, and trying her best to act like everything was normal. Inside, though, adrenaline was pouring into her bloodstream and she felt like she could sprint a mile.

"Are you okay?" Julia asked for at least the second time since Emery had come to pick her up for lunch. "You're distracted."

It'd been three weeks since they ran into Amanda Drake in the hospital hallways, leading to her confession and Kyle Brogan's. Three weeks since Julia told the chief about her problems with her ex, and they'd been living on pins and needles ever since.

Waiting.

Watching.

Expectant.

At once hoping that Samantha stayed far away, and that she just made a damn move already so that the interminable waiting could end.

Emery couldn't take much more of it, being followed around all the time by a police officer and worrying about Julia every minute she wasn't with her. So for the past week, Emery had been keeping a secret.

"Is it unforgivable?" she'd asked Monica when she decided to act. "Is it the dumbest idea I've ever had?"

"Maybe," Monica had answered, a sympathetic look on her face. "But it's also kind of... I don't know, chivalrous?"

Emery still didn't know if what she was doing was catastrophically stupid, but she'd spent the last week getting it all in order and pulling a few strings to make sure it worked. And now she wasn't sure if she'd be able to get through it without her heart pounding out of her chest.

She definitely belonged in a lab, not out on the streets setting up sting operations.

"Hello?"

"Hmm?"

"I asked you a question," Julia said, nudging Emery's arm.

"What was it?"

Julia pulled her to a stop on the sidewalk outside the diner. "Okay, you're starting to really worry me. I asked if you were okay."

"Yeah, I'm fine," Emery said, pushing the door open for her. "Just hungry."

They went in and grabbed a booth – one that Emery strategically steered Julia to because it had a good view of the door. A server came over and got their drink order, and instead of picking up her menu, Julia kicked Emery lightly beneath the table.

"Are you *sure* you're okay? You're not planning to like... propose or anything, are you?"

"At the diner on your lunch break?" Emery asked. "Please. Number one, we haven't even hit our two-month-iversary, and I love you but I'm not eager to scare you off by popping the question that fast. And number two, give me some credit. This is not the setting I would choose."

A subtle smile tugged at Julia's lips. "So you've thought about it? Us getting engaged?"

Emery kicked her back. "You have too. You were talking about renting a house together the other day in bed."

"I hate the apartment complex life," Julia said. "Besides, your walls are getting pretty full. I'd love to see you decorating a whole new space with your spider web art."

"Our art," Emery grinned.

She'd taken Julia out to a park near the precinct the previous week to show her how it was done. The park wasn't nearly as good as an undisturbed wooded area for finding spider webs, but she wasn't about to take Julia out into the forest with her ex still at large.

Hopefully that wouldn't be a problem anymore after this meal – if everything went according to plan.

"Just a second," she said as they arrived at their usual booth. "I forgot to send an important email to my boss."

She stepped away from the table and took out her phone. Her heart was still hammering as she opened Facebook and checked in at the diner – mentioning Julia in the post using her old name.

She'd delete it as soon as all this was done, and tell Julia what she did... for now, she was laying a trap. She'd been thinking of what the chief said in his office – that it'd be entrapment if the police were involved. But if it was just Emery masterminding the scheme...

Julia didn't deserve to spend the rest of her life in fear that her psycho ex would show up when she least expected it. So Emery was doing something about it.

"Get that email sent?" Julia asked when Emery returned to the table. A single arched eyebrow told her that Julia did not buy the email cover story.

"Yep, now I can enjoy lunch." Emery slid into the booth across from her, making sure she had a clear view of the door.

Both of their plainclothes police officers were outside the diner. But Julia said the chief was talking about easing back on the security – it'd been three weeks after all, and those cops were needed elsewhere. And that was exactly why this had to happen today.

Come on, Samantha, show your miserable face, Emery thought as she picked up her menu. It wasn't like she was in the mood to eat with her heart in her throat, but she'd have to keep up a pretense of normalcy so neither Julia nor Sam suspected the trap.

"I think I'm gonna get a turkey club today," Julia said.

"Sounds good."

"With onion rings because what the heck, it's almost the weekend."

"Uh-huh."

"Slathered in fish sauce."

Emery's eyes snapped back to Julia. "Excuse me?"

She laughed. "Just seeing if you were paying attention. You expecting someone?"

"No."

"You're staring at the door pretty hard."

"Sorry. I just can't get used to having a cop follow me around all the time," Emery fibbed. "I was wondering if he ever gets a lunch break."

Julia nudged her foot under the table. "You better get used to having a cop around because you're stuck with me now."

They ordered their food, and a few more customers came and went. No sign of Samantha, though, whose face Emery had been able to memorize thanks to social media. She'd sent Sam a friend request a week ago, and made sure to post a photo of herself with Julia so Sam would accept it.

At first she worried the woman would see right through her plan. Why would someone who knew Julia, and presumably knew her history with Samantha, friend request her?

It turned out not to be an issue, though. Sam had immediately accepted and left a comment on Emery's profile photo about how pretty Julia looked. It turned

Emery's stomach, but from there, it was just a matter of luring her closer, tempting her to make her move and then choosing the moment.

But where was she?

Emery had been sure this would work. Maybe Sam was smarter than she seemed.

"I have good news," Julia said when their food arrived.

"Oh yeah?"

"I think Renee and I have finally worked out a truce," she said, biting into her sandwich. "We're not besties yet, but after I explained why I had to change my name, she looked up my work history in Grand Rapids. She finally believes I'm not hiding some big, horrible secret in my past."

"As she should, you're great at your job," Emery said. "Sounds to me like she's got some baggage of her own."

"Yeah, we haven't gotten into that yet," Julia shrugged. "Maybe someday. Oh, that reminds me, Taphouse tomorrow night? There's been some hinting that it's supposed to be an eventful one."

"Why's that?"

"We think Arlen's finally gonna pop the question."

"At the bar?"

"It's where they fell for each other," Julia explained. "It's sweet."

Emery filed that little tidbit away for the future, and tried not to stare so hard at the door. They finished their lunch, still with no sign of Samantha, and Emery's heart was finally starting to beat at a normal rate. It was frustrating that this meant the waiting had to continue, but she was a little relieved the conflict wasn't going to happen right now.

"I gotta go back," Julia said, checking the time. "Break's almost over. Dinner at my place or yours?"

"Mine, I'll cook," Emery promised. She stood, and her bladder gave a warning pang. "Got time to wait just a minute? I need to use the restroom."

"Sure, I'll take care of the check."

Emery headed for the hallway that led to the single-stall restroom at the back of the diner. She really did have to pee, but she wasn't about to leave Julia alone right now. It occurred to her belatedly that stalkers didn't necessarily like conflict any more than she did, and Sam might not approach Julia while she was with someone.

So Emery stood at the end of the hallway, her back to the dining room, using her phone camera to peek at Julia alone in the booth.

How long should she wait?

How long until Julia got worried and came looking for her?

She was just about to give up when the bell above the diner door jingled and in walked a tall, lanky woman with her bleached strawberry-blonde hair in a messy bob around her face. *Samantha.*

Emery's heart was instantly in her throat again.

She turned around, abandoning the pretense of the phone camera, and watched Samantha make a beeline for Julia's booth. Emery had her phone to her ear, speed-dialing her assigned police officer, but Julia's was already coming through the door.

"Hey," he barked at Sam.

Julia's head shot up and she locked eyes with her ex. Emery saw absolute terror in her expression, and in that instant, she hated that she'd done this. She set this up, she made Julia feel this way.

"Franny," Sam said, looking desperate.

"Freeze," the officer demanded, "you're under arrest for violating a restraining order."

Julia was pressed up against the back of the booth like a scared animal, and Emery practically vaulted across the room to be at her side. The second Sam spotted her, her eyes narrowed. "You tricked me!"

"I had no choice," Emery said, staring right back at her. She *maybe* would not have been so brave if two armed police officers weren't present, but brave or not, she knew she'd do anything to protect Julia.

"You did this?" she asked.

The officer was in the process of cuffing Sam's wrists. Emery hugged Julia tight, and the whole diner was in a commotion. Now wasn't the time for details – that would come later. Instead, she just said, "I had to keep you safe."

Julia buried her face against Emery's shoulder, squeezing her fiercely. "I love you so much."

Behind them, Sam screamed. It was an ear-piercing sound that made Julia wince in Emery's arms. "No, you love *me!*"

She started to struggle, writhing in the officer's grasp. The second one came through the door to assist, and

Emery held Julia tighter. There was a very satisfying moment when Sam thrashed so hard she gave the cops no choice but to slam her down and pin her on a tabletop.

"You're *mine,* Franny," she was mumbling, her mouth smashed against the laminate. "You don't love her, you love me."

Julia looked at her, never letting go of Emery. "No, I don't. I never did, do you hear that?"

Sam looked like she'd just taken a bullet to the chest. Her expression cracked wide open, and she limply allowed the officers to haul her back upright. Julia took a step toward her ex.

"Wait," she told the cops. They held Sam tightly and Julia approached her. "We're finished. There's nothing left between us, and you're going to leave me *and* my partner alone now. You got that?"

"Fran–"

"*Do you hear me?*" Julia insisted.

Sam nodded, defeated.

"Take her away," Julia told the officers.

They went outside to watch Sam being loaded into a squad car that was now waiting for her. As it pulled away from the curb and made the short trip up the street to the precinct, Emery put her arm around Julia's shoulders.

"Do you think she'll listen?"

Julia sighed. "God, I hope so. If she didn't hear me, then the charges I'm about to press will reinforce the message." She turned to Emery. "I can't believe you got my ex arrested."

"In a lot of other circumstances, that'd be a red flag."

"In ours, it's a very, very good sign," Julia said. "It means we can officially start our life together, no more baggage getting in the way."

"I'd carry your baggage all over the world for you, babe."

EPILOGUE

JULIA

On Friday night, Julia was still floating on the knowledge that her stalker ex was behind bars and no threat to anyone. Her first case for Fox County was closed, and she'd just been assigned a new one that looked like gang violence, but with enough strange details that she was going to have to challenge herself to put the pieces together. And she was walking into the Taphouse on the arm of the hottest lab geek in the world.

In short, life was beautiful and she was ready to celebrate that fact.

"What are you drinking tonight, babe?" Emery asked as they neared the bar.

"I don't think it's too early for a shandy, do you?" Julia asked.

It wasn't quite summer yet, but the trees had their leaves again and the air was turning warm outside. It meant Emery would soon have lots of time for her research while the students were on summer break, and it also meant Julia had been enjoying Emery in short-sleeve shirts, her long, lean muscles on display.

"Be right back," she said, and Julia watched her weave her way to the bar.

She was standing there with what was probably a pretty slack-jawed look on her face, admiring her own woman, when Renee and Tate bumped up against her.

"Scoop your jaw off the floor, we get it – your girlfriend is hot," Renee said.

Julia laughed, making a show of closing her mouth with her hand. "We've had an eventful week and I guess I was just appreciating how lucky I got with that one. She took me to meet her best friend already."

"That's sweet," Tate said.

"Is it the same rules as for parents, if they don't hate you just a little, it's a bad sign?" Renee asked.

"Nah, I think the three of us are going to get along just fine."

Emery joined them with the promised summer shandy, and they all found a table where they could wait for the others to join them.

"You two get any interesting cases this week?" Julia asked.

"Nothing too big, investigating a dealer cutting his junk with fentanyl and not telling anybody," Tate said with her jaw tight. "Creep."

"I just finished my part in the skeleton-in-the-tree case," Renee said, and everyone perked up.

"Oh yeah, what's the verdict?" Julia asked. There was still a very slight twinge of jealousy whenever that case came up – especially because Renee got it – but if she'd worked that case, she might never have grown close to Emery. And she wouldn't trade her new girlfriend for all the fascinating cases in the world.

"Forensic anthropologist finished examining the bones just the other day," Renee said. "There were no marks on the skeleton to indicate cause or manner of death."

"Damn," Tate said. "So it's open?"

"Yeah, and I've exhausted every missing persons resource available," Renee said. "He's John Doe unless something changes."

The rest of the group trickled in slowly over the next hour, until there were so many of them they had to pull three tables together. There were women from all areas of the police department, plus a good showing from the medical examiner's office, and a few partners like Emery who didn't share the work connection. There were Tom and Christopher, the only two male members of the group. And Julia counted herself damn lucky to be assimilated so readily into it.

She'd only been in Fox County for six weeks now, but already she'd found the love of her life here, proved herself as a detective, and made a brand-new set of friends.

Plus, Sam was looking at up to six months in jail for her little appearance at the diner, and maybe – just maybe – that'd be enough to teach her the lesson she so desperately needed to learn. Even if Julia had to deal with her again in the future, Sam had done her a favor by driving her out of Michigan. She'd started Julia on the path that led her to this moment.

Julia grabbed Emery's hand, kissing her knuckles.

"What was that for?"

"Just because."

Everybody was keeping their eyes on the bar's entrance, waiting for Arlen and Maya to arrive. Nobody knew what Arlen had in mind – would the proposal happen right at the beginning of the night? Would she wait until it was time to go home? Did she have something special cooked up?

Would she chicken out yet again?

When they finally did come through the doors, everyone immediately turned their attention back to the table, conspicuously avoiding Arlen and Maya's gaze like they hadn't been waiting with bated breath for close to an hour.

"How about those Phillies?" Tate said. "I hear they're supposed to have a good team this year."

Emery laughed. "I'm so far from being a sportsball person that I couldn't even tell you what sport we're talking about."

Tate raised an eyebrow. "Haven't you lived in PA a while?"

"My whole life," Emery answered proudly.

Arlen approached the table while Maya headed to the bar to get their first round of drinks. She slid onto the barstool next to Julia and said, "Way to act natural, all of you. I could see you staring at us from across the room."

"We told Julia a couple weeks ago when she wanted

to bring Emery to the bar for the first time, and we'll tell you now," Renee said. "Subtlety is not our strong suit, so you better act fast."

"Do *not* rush this woman," one of the investigators from the ME's office said. "We'll be waiting another six months for the proposal."

"Hush!" Arlen hissed as Maya weaved her way closer through the crowd. "Not a word, any of you."

"We're just giving you a hard time," Tom said. "You'll go at your own pace, we know that. And you can trust us."

"Sure, I can." Arlen rolled her eyes. "Hey, babe."

Maya sat down next to Arlen, setting two snifters on the table. One was filled to the brim with a reddish-pink mixed drink and topped with a sprig of mint. The other had about half an inch of caramel-brown liquor in it.

"What's this, are they out of beer?"

Maya laughed. "I asked the bartender to whip us up something special for a change. Barrel-aged nine-year-old bourbon, neat. Try it."

"Can I have the other one instead? Looks more my speed," Arlen said, reaching for the more frilly of the two.

Maya slapped her hand away playfully. "Expand your palate. I picked that out for you, it was expensive."

"Well, I hate to disappoint you when I choke on it," Arlen said, but she picked up the snifter in front of her. Everyone at the table was watching and she made a show of taking a sip. Her face reddened and it was clear she was losing a battle with high-test alcohol. She swallowed, then stuck her tongue out, her voice hoarse. "Okay, babe,

I love you but that tastes like rubbing alcohol to me. Sorry."

"Okay," Maya said with a sigh. "I was just trying to get you out of your comfort zone. Try this one instead – it's called a Cupid's Kiss. Blood orange liqueur, Sprite, muddled berries, all the sweet stuff you like."

"Mmm, that sounds more like it," Arlen said, but as soon as her hand closed around the small stem of the glass, she froze.

Maya was grinning from ear to ear. "Something wrong, sweetie?"

"What's this?" Arlen asked. There was a slim white ribbon looped around the stem, and tied to it was a ring.

The entire table was dead-silent. The bar around them all was bustling with activity, but amongst their little group, no one even breathed. Emery slid off her stool and stepped behind Julia, encircling her in her arms.

"What's it look like?" Maya asked.

Arlen put her head in her hands. "Babe, are you proposing to me?"

"Well, I didn't think you'd react like that!" Maya had her arms around Arlen's shoulders, nuzzling against her cheek as she spoke. "What's wrong? The drink thing was a ruse, I knew you'd want the Cupid's Kiss–"

"I was going to propose to *you!*" Arlen groaned. "Tonight!"

"Seriously?" Maya asked.

"Seriously!" pretty much everyone around the table agreed in unison.

Arlen took a ring box out of the crossbody bag she

had slung over her shoulder. "There's a band coming in about an hour, they're gonna have live music here tonight. I begged them to play 'Make You Feel My Love' – remember that song came on in the car the first time we DDed together and I played chauffeur for everybody?"

"I remember," Maya said, tears in her eyes.

"I fucked it up," Arlen said. "I was going to propose to you *months* ago and I just kept chickening out, and now you beat me to it. I am so sorry, babe."

Maya caught Arlen's face in her hands, kissing her and looking her in the eyes. "You didn't fuck anything up. I love you."

"I love you too," Arlen said, sounding hopeless. "Do you want the ring?"

Maya put her hand over the box before Arlen could open it. "Yes, but not yet. I want to finish my proposal, and later tonight when they play that Bob Dylan song, I want you to do your proposal. Who says we can't have two?"

Arlen's expression softened and she tucked the ring box safely back into her bag.

"So, Arlen Rose, will you do me the honor of becoming my wife?" Maya asked, untying her ring from the stem of the glass and presenting it.

"I would love nothing more," Arlen answered, and the table erupted into cheers. When strangers around the bar caught wind of what was happening, they started applauding Maya and Arlen too, and Julia felt Emery's arms tighten around her.

"That was so sweet," she said into Julia's ear. "Is it too soon to say I can't wait til it's our turn?"

"Maybe a little, but I feel the same," Julia answered, turning to pull Emery into a kiss. "Everyone who just got done clapping will be so confused when the same two women get engaged an hour from now," she laughed when the kiss finally ended. She looked over to see Maya and Arlen still going at it.

Then she felt a buzz against her hip and jumped.

"That's me," Emery apologized, taking out her phone. "Monica..." She answered it, and Julia watched her face go from concentrating to hear over the bar noise to panicked. When she hung up, she said, "Monica's having her baby! I promised I'd be at the hospital with her in case her husband drove her insane or passed out or something. I'm going to have to miss proposal number two, I'm so sorry."

"We'll ask someone to video it," Julia said, sliding off her barstool.

"You're coming with me?"

Julia grinned. "I'd go anywhere with you. Just lead the way."

The End

ALSO BY CARA MALONE

Read the five-book first season of Fox County Forensics, starting with Mind Games, featuring a rookie forensic investigator, a seasoned patrol officer, and a crime scene that might just be the death of them both.

Read it now in Kindle Unlimited

ANGEL OF MERCY

FOX COUNTY BOOK 7

Coming September 2023 – Don't miss it, preorder now on Amazon

Printed in Great Britain
by Amazon